Opening a few years after the end of World War II and covering almost a quarter-century, here is comics master Osamu Tezuka's most direct and sustained critique of Japan's fate in the aftermath of total defeat. Unusually devoid of cartoon premises yet shot through with dark voyeuristic humor, *Ayako* looms as a pinnacle of Naturalist literature in Japan with few peers even in prose, the striking heroine a potent emblem of things left unseen following the war.

The year is 1949. Crushed by the Allied Powers, occupied by General MacArthur's armies, Japan has been experiencing massive change. Agricultural reform is dissolving large estates and redistributing plots to tenant farmers—terrible news, if you're landowners like the archconservative Tenge family. For patriarch Sakuemon, the chagrin of one of his sons coming home alive from a POW camp instead of having died for the Emperor is topped only by the revelation that another of his is consorting with "the Reds." What solace does he have but his youngest Ayako, apple of his eye, at once daughter and granddaughter?

Delving into some of the period's true mysteries, which remain murky to this day, Tezuka's Zolaesque tapestry delivers thrill and satisfaction in spades. Another page-turning classic from an irreplaceable artist who was as astute an admirer of the Russian masters and Nordic playwrights as of Walt Disney, *Ayako* is a must-read for comics connoisseurs and curious literati.

Translation - Mari Morimoto
Production - Hiroko Mizuno
        Glen Isip
        Rina Nakayama
        Christine Lee
        Grace Lu
        Nicole Dochych

Published by Vertical, Inc., New York

Originally serialized in Japanese as *Ayako* in *Biggu Komikku*, Shogakkan, 1972-73.

ISBN: 978-1-935654-78-0

Manufactured in the United States of America

First Paperback Edition

Second Printing

This is a work of fiction.
The artwork of the original has been produced as a mirror-image
in order to conform with the English language.

Vertical, Inc.
451 Park Avenue South, 7th Floor
New York, NY 10016
www.vertical-inc.com

AYAKO

OSAMU TEZUKA

VERTICAL.

TABLE OF CONTENTS

CHAPTER 1

HOMECOMING

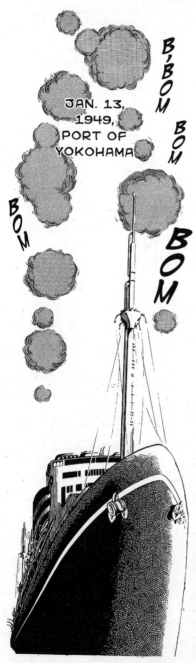

9

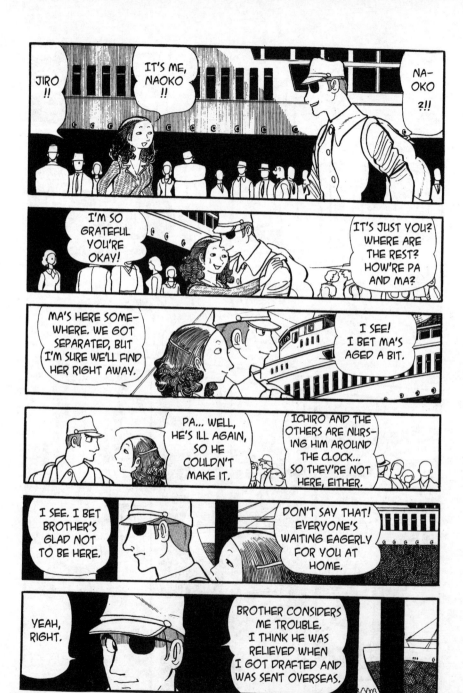

10

NOTE: WHILE PHONETICALLY A COMMON NAME, HERE AND THROUGHOUT AYAKO IS SPELLED WITH A CHARACTER THAT MEANS "ODD."

WHOSE, THEN?!

I'LL TELL YOU LATER...

HEY, THERE'S THIS PLACE I WANT TO STOP BY BEFORE WE HEAD HOME...

YASU-KUNI SHRINE?

NOPE... I'LL NEED ABOUT 2 HOURS. WAIT FOR ME SOME-WHERE?

OUR TRAIN LEAVES AT 5:30. CAN YOU GET TO UENO BY THEN?

WE'LL WAIT FOR YOU THERE.

THERE'S A CHINESE EATERY, "KIYOH," NEAR THE STATION.

YA MAKE IT SOUND EASY, BUT WON'T JIRO GET LOST 'N WANDER 'ROUND IN CIRCLES?

13

COME IN.

15

YOU PASS.

YOU WERE AT THE 22ND INTERNMENT CAMP NEAR MANILA. DO YOU KNOW COLONEL RESTON?

YES... THE COLONEL IS THE ONE WHO...

COL. RESTON WAS AN ACADEMY CLASSMATE OF MY BOSS, MAJ. GEN. WILLOUGHBY.

YOU'RE TREATED SPECIAL. THEY MUST TRUST YOU.

AND MY TASK?

YOU'LL BE TOLD LATER.

MAKE SURE TO LEAVE US YOUR CONTACT INFO.

A WORD OF WARN- ING.

DON'T GET TOO CHUMMY WITH THE GOVERN- MENT SECTION FELLAS.

BUT...

I THOUGHT GOVSEC WAS PART OF HQ?

GOVSEC IS GOVSEC, AND WE ARE GENERAL STAFF OFFICE, SECTION 2! THERE ARE THINGS EACH OF US DOESN'T WANT THE OTHER TO KNOW.

OH... AND ONE MORE THING.

CIVVIES OUGHTN'T BOLDLY STROLL IN AND OUT THE FRONT ENTRANCE.

FOLKS LIKE YOU ESPECIALLY. SLINK THROUGH THE BACK DOOR.

GOOD LUCK

HEY, YOU. YOU KNOW THAT JAP WHO STUCK HIS NECK OUT THE DOOR EARLIER?

YEAH... WE WERE WAR BUDDIES.

I WAS DEMOBILIZED FIRST.

HIS NAME'S TENGE.

IT'S MOST UNFORTUNATE, THAT YOU HAPPENED TO SEE THIS MAN...

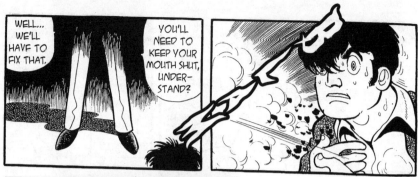

WELL... WE'LL HAVE TO FIX THAT.

YOU'LL NEED TO KEEP YOUR MOUTH SHUT, UNDER- STAND?

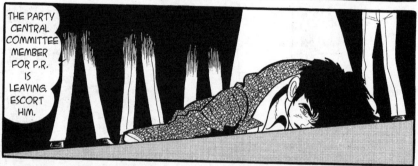

THE PARTY CENTRAL COMMITTEE MEMBER FOR P.R. IS LEAVING. ESCORT HIM.

WOOO-OO-I-OOO

EH... HMM?

HMM?

IT'S JIRO, PA, JIRO!

JIRO, EY...

WHY'JA COME HOME?

WHY DIDN'JA DIE, FER OUR MOTHER-LAND?!

I AIN' GREETIN' YA!

'N I AIN' GOT A SINGLE FIELD T'GIVE YA, NEITHER!

PA!

I DON' WANNA SEE YER MUG. SCAT!

WHAT ARE YA SAYIN' TO OUR POOR SON... CAN'T YA AT LEAST THANK 'IM FER HIS TROUBLES?

OH, 'N THERE'S AYAKO. SHIRO'S LI'L SISTER.

AYAKO'S QUITE THE APPLE OF PA'S EYE.

24

WHOSE CHILD IS SHE, MA?!

SHADDUP!!

...

NOW, JIRO, ICHIRO AND HIS WIFE ARE IN THE BACK ROOM... GO ON ALONG.

ICHIRO, SIS, I HAVE JUST RETURNED.

NOTE: O-RYO IS SINGING THE FIRST VERSE OF "TOSA NO SUNAYAMA (THE SAND DUNES OF TOSA)," AN O-BON DANCE FOLK SONG OF AOMORI PREFECTURE.

CHAPTER 2

THE *IWAI-DEN*

JAN. 30, 1949

CAW CAW CAW CAW

28

LET US FEAST!

FATHER

AGED, BUT THE SAME AS EVER ...

SAKUEMON TENGE, AGE 52. MAJOR LANDOWNER, ARROGANT, GRANDIOSE, DEBAUCHED, LECHEROUS, RUDE, SKEPTICAL, AND A MACHIAVELLIAN. A THOROUGHLY CONTEMPTIBLE HUMAN BEING...

YET NOT A SINGLE MEMBER OF HIS SIZEABLE FAMILY STANDS UP TO HIM. IS IT FROM FEAR? OR RESIGNA- TION?

MOTHER... IBA TENGE, AGE 51.

THE VERY MODEL OF A SELFLESSLY DEVOTED, VIRTUOUS WIFE ...

BIG BROTHER ICHIRO TENGE, AGE 27. A CALCULATING OPPORTUNIST, SHAM MORALIST, AND FATHER'S WILY ASSOCIATE.

NOTE: THE NAME TENGE USES CHARACTERS FOR "HEAVEN" AND "OUTSIDE," SUGGESTING A CERTAIN FORSAKENNESS.

SIS-IN-LAW SU'E, AGE 23. A RETICENT AND FAIRLY NIHILISTIC WOMAN WHO LOOKS OLDER THAN HER YEARS, AROUND WHOM HANGS A CLOUD OF SADNESS.

LITTLE SISTER NAOKO, AGE 18. HIGH SCHOOL STUDENT. AN ORDINARY GIRL WITH A CHEERY PERSONALITY I FIND AGREEABLE. LOVED BY EVERYONE.

LITTLE BROTHER SHIRO, AGE 12. GRADE SCHOOL STUDENT. THE MOST CLEAR-HEADED MEMBER OF OUR FAMILY, QUITE THE THEORIST. WHEN FIXED BY HIS GAZE, EVEN BIG BROTHER ICHIRO WILL FIDGET AND YIELD.

AND AYAKO... AGE 4.

LITTLE SISTER? OR...

...NIECE?

MOTHER'S ODD BEWILDER- MENT... PLUS, IS A SPITTING IMAGE OF SIS-IN-LAW.

31

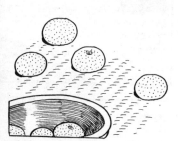

GOOD MEAL.

THUMP THUMP THUMP

JIRO, I NEED TO TALK TO YOU, ALONE.

SURE.

MASTA, ME SAWS IT!

YER LADY-WIFE...

AIEE!!

O-RYO! GO AWAY, SCAT!!

AYE...

THAT WAS A BIT HARSH TOWARDS A HALF-WIT, BROTHER.

LET'S GO TO THE IWAI-DEN, JIRO. HAVE YOU PAID YOUR RESPECTS YET SINCE RETURN-ING?

33

THE *IWAI-DEN*—
MINI-SHRINES FOUND
ON FARMLANDS.
IN THE YODOYAMA
REGION, AND ACROSS
CHUBU AND KANTO,
THE FOX-DEITY
INARI AND MOUNTAIN
GODS RATHER THAN
ANCESTRAL SPIRITS
ARE VENERATED AS
CLAN GUARDIANS.
SAID TO BE THE
PRIMITIVE FORM OF
VILLAGE TUTELARIES.

34

SEE THAT, JIRO? LANDS THAT WERE OURS WHEN YOU WERE A BOY HAVE ALL PASSED INTO THE HANDS OF TENANT FARMERS! THERE, THERE TOO, AND EVEN THERE!

IT'S ALL THE AMERICANS' DOING...

SNAP

THE YEAR THE WAR ENDED, THE GOVERNMENT ABRUPTLY ISSUED AN AGRICULTURAL LAND REFORM ACT... LANDOWNERS HOLDING MORE THAN 12.5 ACRES HAD TO RELEASE LAND TO FARMERS... OUR TENANT FARMERS DANCED WITH GLEE.

ON ITS HEELS CAME THE SPECIAL MEASURES ACT OF 2 YEARS AGO. LANDOWNERS COULD ONLY OWN 2.5 ACRES OF LEASE LAND... HUMPH!

SO THE GOVERN-MENT'S BOUGHT UP ABOUT 30,000 ACRES. PRIOR TO THAT, FARMERS' COOPERATIVES FORMED AND STARTED A RUCKUS...

SNAP

THEY'VE GONE OVER TO THE REDS...

35

IT CAN'T BE HELPED, BROTHER. LOSERS DON'T GET TO CALL THE SHOTS.

YOU SAY THAT, BUT I'VE CRIED FROM THE FRUSTRATION.

OUR FAMILY'S IN TERRIBLE STRAITS. PA'S WITHERING AWAY AND EVEN HAD A TOMB MADE. HE'LL PROBABLY CEDE AS FAMILY HEAD TO ME SOON.

I'M GOING TO BE BLUNT, JIRO... THERE AREN'T ANY ASSETS SET ASIDE FOR YOU.

...

I...TRIED TO INTERCEDE ON YOUR BEHALF, BUT PA SAID A MAN TAKEN POW INSTEAD OF DYING NOBLY SHAN'T PARTAKE IN HIS ESTATE... HE'S SO OBSTINATE...

IS MY COMING HOME A NUISANCE TO YOU TOO, BROTHER?

OH NO, I...

I THOUGHT ABOUT THIS A LOT, AND I'VE FOUND YOU A NICE AND EASY BUT WORTHWHILE JOB.

YOU'D HEAD THE OFFICE OF A WAREHOUSE IN KOBINATA TOWNSHIP. IT'S A BIT FAR FROM HERE, BUT YOU'LL BE ABLE TO STAY HOME ON THE WEEKENDS.

THAT'S ALL RIGHT, BRO-THER.

I'LL FIND MY OWN JOB. I DON'T WANT TO BE A BURDEN TO YOU.

PHEW

BUT THERE ARE STILL A LOT OF THINGS I DON'T UNDER-STAND.

LIKE AYAKO...

WHAT ABOUT AYAKO?!!

MA GAVE BIRTH TO HER AT 47!

DID I TICK YOU OFF, BROTHER?

WHAT'S THIS?

SO MUCH GRAFFITI! WHO'D DO THAT TO A SHRINE?

HEY THERE, MISTER TANAKA!

...

SHEESH... IS IT REALLY THAT TERRIBLE THAT I WAS A POW?

THE VILLAGE HAS BEEN SNUBBING ME THESE PAST **2** WEEKS.

THE STORE-HOUSE DOOR'S OPEN.

?

THAT'S SIS-IN-LAW AND PA!

JUST AS I SUS-PECT-ED...

HAH... HAH...

AH!

KLUNK

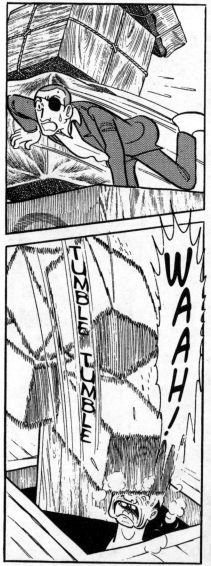

IT AIN'T LIKE IT JUST STARTED RECENTLY... HE BEEN LIKE THAT SINCE HE WERE YOUNG.

WHAT, DIDN'T START RE-CENTLY?!

AM I YOUR CHILD, MA?

WHY DOES EVERYONE TALK SHAME-LESSLY ABOUT THIS?

WE'RE A WARPED FAMILY!!

THEY'RE ALL INSANE!!

THIS MIGHT BE MORE THAN YOU WANT TO KNOW, BUT ICHIRO OFFERED UP SIS-IN-LAW IN EXCHANGE FOR PA'S ENTIRE ESTATE.

ON PA'S DE-MANDS.

WHAP!!

44

EVERY NOW AND THEN, SHE ENRAGES ME FOR NO REASON...

FORGIVE ME...

WELL, NO WONDER! SHE'S HALF OUR SISTER AND HALF YOUR CHILD!

...

SEEING PA OR BROTHER'S FACE MAKES ME SICK.

THE 500-YEAR HISTORY OF THE TENGE FAMILY WILL NOW END...

I NEVER SHOULD HAVE COME HOME.

JIRO TENGE, WHAT ABOUT YOU?

...ME?

WHAT DO YOU MEAN?

DO YOU REALLY THINK YOU'RE AN EXCEPTION?

45

I SWEAR BY HEAVEN, EARTH, AND THE GODS...

WHAT ABOUT THE COLONEL RESTON MATTER?

DO YOU ADMIT THAT YOU WERE A SPY?

AT THE MANILA POW CAMP, HOW MANY COUNTRYMEN DID YOU BETRAY IN ORDER TO CURRY FAVOR WITH THE WARDEN?

I HAD TO DO THAT TO SURVIVE!!

HYPO-CRITE!

RIDICU-LOUS!!

YOU'RE A COWARDLY TRAITOR.

YOU THINK YOU HAVE THE RIGHT TO CONDEMN YOUR FAMILY?

DO YOU ADMIT THAT YOU'RE A BIGGER FOOL AND LOSER THAN YOUR FATHER OR BROTHER?

BRO-BRO, WHACHA THINKING?

SHUT UP!

CHAPTER 3

THE MAN CALLED KATO

JIRO BRO, COME PLAY WITH ME? YOU TOO, AYAKO.

WHAT ARE YOU UP TO NOW?

A MOCK TRIAL.

MOCK TRIAL? IS THAT WHAT KIDS THESE DAYS DO FOR FUN, SHIRO?

IT'S REAL POPULAR AT SCHOOL.

YOU AND AYAKO ARE THE ACCUSED, SO SIT THERE.

THE ACCUSED ...? NASTY ROLES. NO LAWYERS?

THOSE DOLLS.

BUT DOLLS CAN'T TALK.

48

THERE'S NO POINT IN HAVING A DEFENSE TEAM ANYWAY, SINCE NONE OF THEIR MOTIONS PASS.

WHAT?

THIS IS THE FAR EAST TRIBUNAL.

THE INTERNATIONAL MILITARY TRIBUNAL COURT IS HEREBY CONVENED TO TRY CLASS A WAR CRIMINALS. THIS COURT SHALL CONFORM TO INTERNATIONAL LAW AND MORALITY, AND ADHERE TO STRICT NEUTRALITY.

WHOA... I'M SHOCKED. WHERE'D YOU LEARN SUCH WORDS?

ACCUSED, ALL STAND!

AYAKO, STAND UP.

LEAD PRO-SECUTOR, YOUR OPENING ARGUMENT.

PURR PURR

PURRR PURRR

   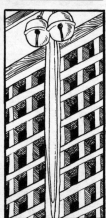

SISTER!!

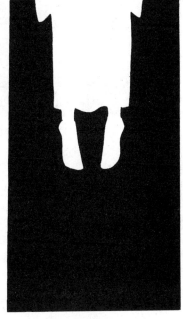

SISTER!!

HOLD ON!

GAG

H-HACK HACK...

GAG

53

BUT I THOUGHT BROTHER ONLY TOLD YOU TO LET PA HAVE HIS WAY WITH YOU ONCE, IN EXCHANGE FOR THE INHERITANCE.

JUST ONCE... RIGHT?

AT FIRST, YES.

BUT FATHER KEPT INSISTING, A THIRD TIME, THEN A FOURTH...

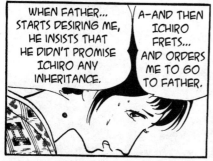

WHEN FATHER... STARTS DESIRING ME, HE INSISTS THAT HE DIDN'T PROMISE ICHIRO ANY INHERITANCE.

A-AND THEN ICHIRO FRETS... AND ORDERS ME TO GO TO FATHER.

AND YOU JUST MEEKLY GO? GIVE ME A BREAK... THAT'S TERRIBLE!

PA IS CRAZY. AND BROTHER SO SERVILE...

YOU'RE A FOOL, SIS!

YOU MUST REFUSE THEM!!

IF I TRY TO STAND UP TO HIM, ICHIRO...

BEATS ME.

THEN YOU OUGHT TO DIVORCE HIM RIGHT AWAY!

AND THEN WHAT? I CAN'T GO BACK TO MY PARENTS... WHERE COULD I GO?

WHAT A FARCE.

I AM JUST APPALLED.

IT'S JUST A GAME, BIG BRO.

DON'T YOU DARE EVER CALL ME A SPY AGAIN, SHIRO!!

WHAT'S THE MATTER, EY? NOW NOW, NO FIGHTIN'.

LOOK NOW, SHIRO'S CRYIN', THE POOR THING.

WE'RE NOT FIGHTING, MA.

AH WELL, YA GOT A LETTER, JIRO.

FROM A FRIEND, I THINK.

...

YEAH, A FRIEND FROM SCHOOL.

I'M HEADING OUT.

SORRY, SHIRO.

GOING INTO TOWN.

I'LL BE OUT LATE, SO I WON'T NEED DINNER.

56

Do you like American movies? On the 10th around 3pm, let's meet at Kobinata's Central Cinema, row E, seat 22. Friend M

Your friend awaits you at 33 First Street. When you arrive, give the code greeting.

DO YOU LIKE AMERICAN MOVIES?

I'VE BEEN EXPECTING YOU.

THIS IS A SINGLE RESIDENCE HOME. DON'T WORRY ABOUT BEING OVERHEARD.

NOTE: CIC = COUNTER-INTELLIGENCE CORPS

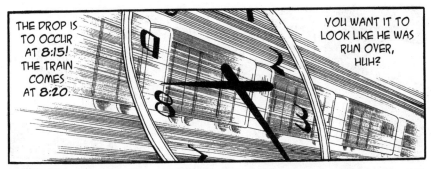

THE DROP IS TO OCCUR AT **8:15!** THE TRAIN COMES AT **8:20.**

YOU WANT IT TO LOOK LIKE HE WAS RUN OVER, HUH?

LEAVE THE SCENE AS SOON AS YOU PLACE THE BODY. DON'T DALLY AND GET SEEN!

THE CAR SHOULD BE DUMPED THERE, TOO.

NOW RECITE THAT BACK TO ME.

AT **6:20**PM ON THE **17**TH, I AM TO TAKE A PASSENGER FROM THE STATION TO A DESIGNATED LOCATION. I WILL LEAVE FOR **30** MINUTES AND THEN RETURN TO DRIVE A CORPSE TO THE SPECIFIED TRACKS BY **8:15.** THE CAR WILL BE LEFT THERE TOO.

GOOD. HERE'S A PICTURE OF THE MARK AND A MAP OF THE DESIGNATED LOCATIONS.

INTRIGUING. THAT'S CERTAINLY A PLACE THAT WON'T BE SEARCHED UNLESS YOU'RE DEAD.

WE'LL PROBABLY NEVER MEET AGAIN.

BE CARE-FUL.

THIS MAN WHO WILL GET OFF THE TRAIN... THAT I WILL GUIDE... AND MOST LIKELY BECOME THE CORPSE. A MAN I'M TO MAKE LOOK LIKE A HIT-BY-TRAIN!

WHO AND WHAT IS HE?

HE MUST BE SOMEONE ON GHQ'S BLACKLIST...

IN NEED OF ERASING ...

BUT WHY WILL HE BE IN A BACK-WOODS TOWN?

62

YOU HAVE A ROOM UPSTAIRS?

WE DO, BUT IT'S RENTED OUT TONIGHT.

OH, I BET. I RENTED IT.

SIR, PLEASE WAIT!

OUR POLICY AS A LOCAL CHAPTER IS TO SUPPORT AND AID THE STRUGGLE.

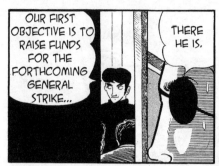

66

ARE THE UPCOMING LAYOFFS REALLY A RESULT OF FINANCIAL PROBLEMS AT THE NATIONAL RAILWAY? I CANNOT BELIEVE THIS IS ENTIRELY JNR'S INSPIRATION.

SO WHAT DO YOU THINK, MISS TENGE?

THAT'S DEFINITELY NAOKO...

SHE'S A MEMBER OF THE DPP?!

MY IMPRESSION OF NAOKO WAS ALWAYS OF A CHEERFUL, HAPPY-GO-LUCKY ORDINARY GIRL WHO'S LOVED BY ALL...

WHEN IN THE WORLD DID SHE TURN RED?

FOR SURE, THE JNR WAS ONLY INAUGURATED THIS MONTH AND IS UNDER PRESSURE TO BE SELF-SUPPORTING.

WE HAVE ALSO HEARD THEIR EXCUSES THAT PERSONNEL LAW REQUIRES THEM TO LET GO TENS OF THOUSANDS.

WHAT I WONDER ...

THAT'S RIDICULOUS! YOU'RE JUMPING AT SHADOWS.

IS WHETHER THIS WAS DECIDED UPON BY OUR GOVERNMENT... OR ORCHESTRATED BY AMERICA.

THE YOSHIDA ADMINISTRATION IS A PUPPET REGIME OF THE OCCUPA- TION, MACARTHUR'S LAPDOGS.

OUR GOVERNMENT UNDERSTANDS THE LEVEL OF UNEASE THAT LAYING OFF 100,000 CITIZENS WOULD CAUSE.

BUT THE OCCUPATION FORCES...

COULD ISSUE SUCH AN ORDER WITHOUT BREAKING A SWEAT, AS A THIRD PARTY.

IT'S TRUE THAT MAC-ARTHUR'S RULE IS ABSOLUTE.

AFTER ALL, ONE WORD FROM HIM CALLED OFF THE 2-1 STRIKE.

HOWEVER, THERE ARE DIFFERENT ISSUES AT PLAY THIS TIME.

I DON'T THINK THE UPCOMING LAYOFFS ARE RELATED TO THE OCCUPATION FORCES' POLICIES.

SNAP

...

SWING

WE THE YODOYAMA CHAPTER WILL SUPPORT THE STRUGGLE THROUGH FUNDRAISING, DISTRIBUTING LEAFLETS AND POSTERS, AND DEMONSTRA-TIONS.

NOTE: THE "2-1 STRIKE" REFERS TO THE GENERAL STRIKE THAT HAD BEEN SCHEDULED FOR FEBRUARY 1, 1947.

SO THE MAN'S A CHAPTER LEADER OF THE DPP.

BUT WHY DOES GHQ NEED TO KILL HIM IN ONE WEEK'S TIME?

PERHAPS HE POSSESSES SOME CRUCIAL INTEL ON GHQ...

IS THAT WHY THEY WANT TO MAKE IT LOOK LIKE HE WAS RUN OVER?

WHY CAN'T THEY KEEP IT SIMPLE?

HERE THEY COME!

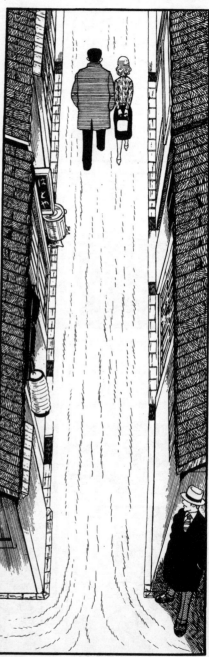

JUNE 16, 1949

HE LAYOFFS

NO ARGUMENTS, MR. SHIMOKAWA! YOU MUST CUT 95,000 EMPLOYEES BY JULY 3RD! NO IFS, ANDS, OR BUTS!

MR. CHAGNON, AT LEAST IN NAME, I AM THE PRESIDENT OF JNR.

I WILL HAVE TO TAKE FULL RESPONSIBILITY FOR ANY MASS LAYOFFS.

OF COURSE YOU DO!!

THUS, I IMPLORE YOU TO ALLOW ME TO DECIDE WHO WILL BE CUT.

YOU WILL CARRY OUT GHQ'S ORDERS DOWN TO THE LETTER! YOU MUST OBEY ME! ME!!

NO!

76

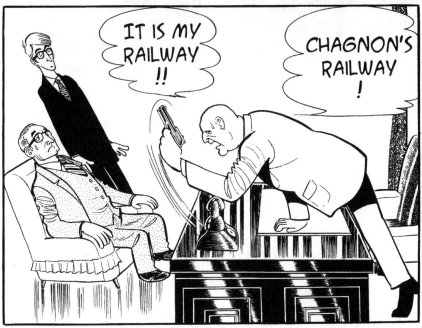

ON JUNE 1ST,
THE JAPANESE NATIONAL
RAILWAYS WAS INAUGURATED.
ITS FIRST PRESIDENT,
NORIYUKI SHIMOKAWA,
PROMOTED FROM VICE-MINISTER
OF TRANSPORT, WAS A LONE WOLF
WITH NO COMRADES OR PROTECTORS
IN THE POLITICAL WORLD.
IT WAS THIS LACK OF COMPLICATED
TIES THAT PROBABLY DREW
GHQ RAILWAYS CHIEF CHAGNON'S
FAVOR.

THE NEWLY INSTALLED
PRESIDENT SHIMOKAWA WAS
IMMEDIATELY PRESSURED
TO LAY OFF 95,000 PEOPLE.
HAVING COME FROM A
RAILWAYS BACKGROUND,
PRESIDENT SHIMOKAWA
CHAFED AT SWALLOWING
HIS ORDERS AS IS.
AND THAT WAS
A DISAPPOINTMENT TO
CHAGNON AND OTHERS...

NOTE: SHIMOKAWA IS CLOSELY MODELED ON SADANORI SHIMOYAMA. ONE OF THE DARKEST
MYSTERIES OF JAPAN'S POSTWAR YEARS, THE "SHIMOYAMA INCIDENT," INVOLVES
HIS FATE.

THE TOKYO-BOUND ON TRACK 1 IS NOW DEPARTING. SENDERS-OFF, PLEASE...

YOU'LL BE BACK TOMORROW?

YEAH. I'M JUST DELIVERING CAMPAIGN FUNDS TO HQ. I'LL BE BACK AROUND 8PM.

WELL THEN, CHAPTER LEADER... HAVE A SAFE TRIP!

HEY... CALL ME BY MY NAME, WILL YOU?

TADASHI... BE CAREFUL!

JIRO!!

YOU LIKE THAT MAN, NAOKO?

Y-YES...

JUNE 17, 1949

I AM MINAGAWA OF THE PARTY'S EXECUTIVE COMMITTEE, HERE TO PICK YOU UP.

AH, MR. MINAGAWA... WE'VE SPOKEN ON THE PHONE.

SHALL WE HEAD STRAIGHT TO HQ?

YES. I'D LIKE TO TAKE CARE OF THIS RIGHT AWAY.

HEY, COULD YOU GIVE HIM A LIFT?

MR. ENO? SURE, HOP IN.

HOW ARE THINGS AT CENTRAL STRIKE HQ?

WELL, EVERY-ONE'S IN QUITE A FRENZY.

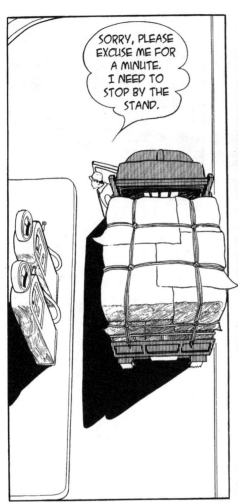

CHAPTER 4

THE FISSURE OF TIME

NOTE: O-RYO IS NOW SINGING "YASABURO-BUSHI," AN ENKA SONG FROM AOMORI.

I GOTS SOMETHIN' T'TELL YA...

FERGET WHACHA SAW IN TH' STOREHOUSE...

IT NEVER HAP-PENED, Y'HEAR?

SURE...

IT'S NONE OF MY BUSINESS, PA.

ICHIRO'S SET T'INHERIT TH' LAND...

BUT IF YER WILLIN' T'KEEP YER EYES CLOSED...

I COULD SET SOMETHIN' ASIDE FER YA...

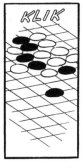
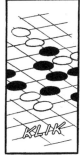

THANKS, PA, AND NOTHING AGAINST ICHIRO, BUT I CAN FIND MY OWN WIFE.

Y-YA TH-TH-THINK I GOTS SOME REASON OF MY OWN P-P-PUSHIN' MARRIAGE ON YA?!

FINE, THEN! I AIN' GIVIN' YA NUTHIN'!

GO!!

FRET FRET

MA, I'M GOING TO NAP. DON'T WAKE ME UNTIL NIGHTTIME, OKAY?

SURE, SURE.

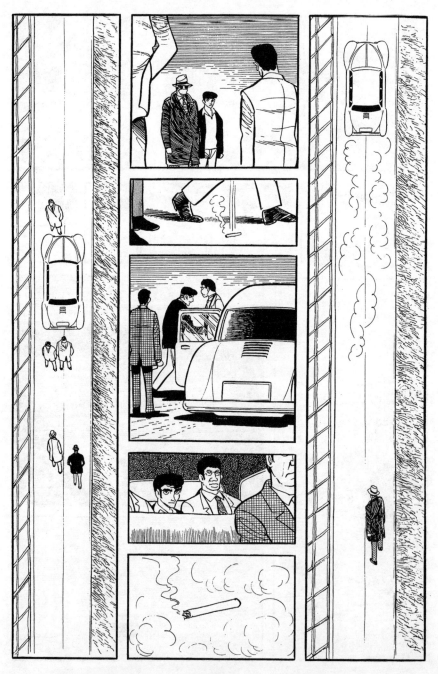

HE'S ICE COLD!

AND ALREADY IN RIGOR.

WHICH MEANS ONE OF THEM'S A STAND-IN.

THIS IS NOT THE MAN I ESCORTED EARLIER!

THEY LOOK ALIKE, BUT IT'S SOMEONE ELSE...

103

UM... WHEN IS THE NEXT OUTBOUND TRAIN DUE?

8:30, MISS.

I THOUGHT HE SAID HE'D BE BACK BY 8PM...

MAYBE HE MISSED HIS TRAIN?

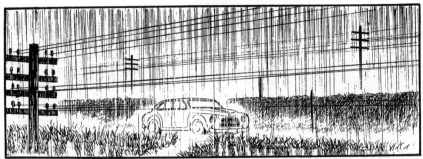

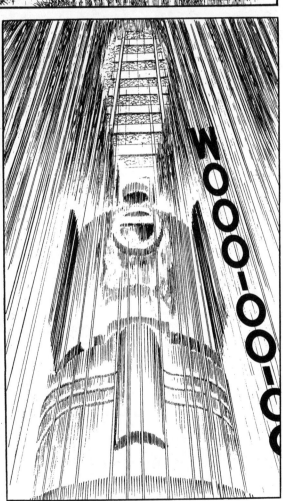

105

106

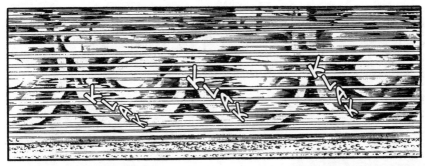

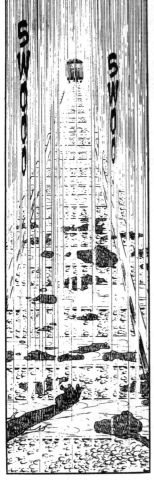

UM, HOW MANY MORE OUTBOUND TRAINS?

THE NEXT IS THE LAST ONE.

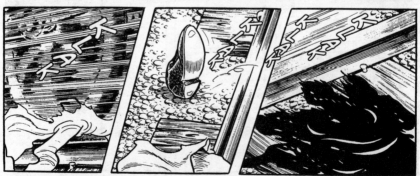

SHOOT!

BLOOD...

SHOULD I THROW THE SHIRT OUT?

IT'LL PROBABLY WASH OFF...

CRAP...

SOAP'S NOT WORKING.

I NEED TO USE GASOLINE OR SOMETHING.

MAYBE TOMORROW?

UHH!!

WHY YA BE DOIN' LAUNDRY SO LATE?

WANT ME T'DO IT?

ME'LL DO...

OY!

THIS BE BLOOD.

O-RYO!! JUST LEAVE IT AND GO! GO, I SAID!

A-AYE...

LISTEN CLOSELY, O-RYO... DO YOU LIKE OR HATE ME?

AH... M-ME LIKES MASTA JIRO, UH-HUH.

THEN YOU LISTEN TO ME, AND IF YOU DO AS I SAY, I'LL BUY YOU SOMETHING YOU WANT.

DON'T TELL ANYBODY ABOUT THIS BLOOD. NOT MY FATHER OR BROTHER, NOT EVEN YOUR PA!

AND NOT ANY VILLAGERS OR SALESMEN, EITHER.

IF YOU KEEP QUIET, I'LL BE SURE TO BUY YOU SOMETHING NICE.

'KAY. ME WANNA K'MONO. WANNA WEAR A K'MONO LIKE DA ONE SUGITA'S WIFEY GOTS.

SURE, SURE, I'LL GET YOU ONE.

NOW GO TO BED.

AND NO TELLING, REMEMBER!

...

113

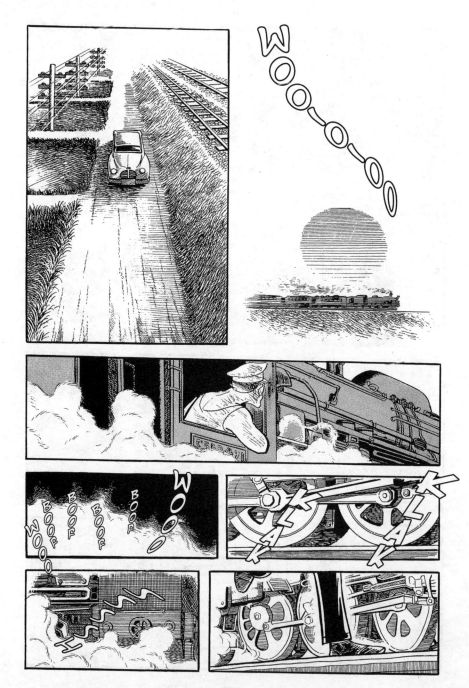

UNUSUAL SEEING A HIT-BY-TRAIN DISMEMBERED THIS BAD.

PROBABLY WENT UNNOTICED DUE TO THE STORM AND WAS STRUCK BY MULTIPLE TRAINS.

I SUSPECT HE WAS RUN OVER BETWEEN 8PM AND THE LAST TRAIN.

ANY EARLIER, AND IT WOULD STILL HAVE BEEN DRY AND BRIGHT ENOUGH FOR AN ENGINEER TO SPOT HIM.

WHAT ABOUT THIS ABANDONED CAR?

THE GROUND'S DRY BENEATH IT, SO IT WAS PARKED PRIOR TO THE RAIN.

WE'VE RETRIEVED HAIRS FROM THE REAR SEATS.

HAVE YOU TRACED THE VEHICLE YET?

IT BELONGS TO NICHIEI FLOUR MILLS' YODOYAMA FACTORY.

AYE, ENO FROM DISTRIBUTION TOOK IT FER A SPIN LAST NIGHT... I WAS JUST PULLIN' ME HAIR OUT 'CUZ HE HADN' BROUGHT IT BACK YET.

ENO ?

AYE, THIS YOUNG FELLA IN DISTRIBUTION ...

TADASHI ENO, HUH ...

WHAT SORT OF CHAP IS HE?

A BACHELOR... 'N COMMITTEE CHAIR O' DA UNION... REAL HARDWORKIN'... LIKED BY EV'RYONE, AYE.

WHAT TIME WAS IT... AND HOW'D HE SEEM WHEN HE DROVE OFF?

HMM... 'TWAS 'BOUT 7:30... CAME IN ALL A SUDDEN FROM DA OUTSIDE, SEEMIN' REAL DOWN FER A CHANGE.

HE APPEARED DEPRESSED?

AYE. I CALLED OUT TO 'IM, BUT HE DIDN' REALLY RESPOND.

HE SAT SLUMPED IN A CHAIR, DEEP IN THOUGHT.

THEN HE STOOD UP, ALL VACANT...

MAY I USE THE CAR?

SURE, GO AHEAD.

HE'S USED IT AFORE T'GO TO DA OFFICE IN TOWN, SO I DIDN' THINK ON IT, MUCH.

HE WENT INTO WORK ON A SUNDAY?

AYE. HE'D BORROW IT SUNDAY EVE TO GO INTO TOWN, 'N RETURN MONDAY...

THIS IS PREFECTURAL HQ. AROUND 7:30 LAST NIGHT, A MAN NAMED ENO OF NICHIEI FLOUR MILLS DEPARTED IN A COMPANY CAR. THAT VEHICLE WAS FOUND ABANDONED BY THE SIDE OF THE JNR TRACKS THIS MORNING. GIVEN THE CIRCUMSTANCES, WE SUSPECT THE DISMEMBERED CORPSE TO BE ENO'S...

PREFECTURAL POLICE HEAD-QUARTERS

BASED ON HIS CLOTHING, SHIRT MONOGRAM, SHOES, AND BLOOD TYPE, WE CAN CONCLUDE THE VICTIM WAS ENO.

県警察局本部

TWO EVENINGS AGO, ENO SET OUT FOR TOKYO. THE PURPOSE OF HIS TRIP WAS TO DELIVER CAMPAIGN FUNDS TO JNR CENTRAL STRIKE HQ.

PATCH ME THROUGH TO TOKYO.

CENTRAL STRIKE HQ CLAIMS ENO NEVER SHOWED UP.

ENO WENT TO TOKYO, BUT TURNED BACK WITHOUT EVER GOING TO HIS DESTINATION. SO WHERE'S THE MONEY?

THERE ARE QUITE A FEW EYEWITNESSES WHO SAW A MAN FITTING ENO'S DESCRIPTION GET OFF THE 6:20 TRAIN LAST NIGHT.

THEY ALL CONFIRM THAT HE WAS WITH A MASKED MAN WEARING DARK GLASSES. HOWEVER, NONE OF THEM COULD STATE WHERE THE TWO PARTED WAYS.

COULD HE BE ANOTHER MEMBER OF DPP'S LOCAL CELL?

THE DISMEMBERED MALE DISCOVERED ON THE JNR LINE HAS BEEN IDENTIFIED AS DPP YODOYAMA CHAPTER LEADER TADASHI ENO. HAVING EXAMINED THE SCENE AND MR. ENO'S MOVEMENTS,

AIEE!

SPECIAL HQ IS RULING OUT NEITHER SUICIDE NOR HOMICIDE.

TADASHI...!

SOB!!

NAOKO... I'M AN EVIL BROTHER!!

WITH THESE HANDS I CARRIED YOUR LOVER'S CORPSE, AND WASHED HIS BLOOD OFF THEM.

IF YOU SHOULD EVER DISCOVER THE TRUTH... FEEL FREE TO KILL ME!

THE POLICE IS LEANING TOWARDS SUICIDE.

NO WAY! IT'S JUST A TRICK.

HE WAS MURDERED BY REACTIONARY ELEMENTS!!

ONE THEORY IS THAT HE KILLED HIMSELF TO TAKE RESPONSIBILITY FOR LOSING THE FUNDS.

MISTER TADASHI ENO

BUT THEN HOW DO YOU EXPLAIN ENO'S HAIR IN THE BACK SEAT OF THE CAR?

I BET HE LAY DOWN IN THE BACK SEAT FOR A WHILE, WITH HIS TROUBLED THOUGHTS, AFTER HE PARKED.

WHICH COULD ALSO EXPLAIN WHY HE TOOK THE EARLIER 6:20 TRAIN BACK INSTEAD OF THE 8PM.

AND THE SCARCITY OF BLOOD ON THE TRACKS?

THE STORM PROBABLY WASHED AWAY THE BLOOD.

IT WASN'T SUICIDE!!

WE WERE SUPPOSED TO MEET UP! HE WOULDN'T DIE WITHOUT SAYING ANYTHING!

THIS WAS A HOMICIDE, I'M SURE OF IT!

THE KILLER IS LAUGHING FROM THE SHADOWS!

WHAT'S WRONG WITH YOU? WE MUST AVENGE HIS DEATH!

OOH, OOH, MASTA JIRO, WHEN YA GONNA BUY ME DAT K'MONO?

SHH!

DAT K'MONO YA PROMISED.

124

WAH!

L-LISTEN UP, O-RYO.

LISTEN REAL CLOSE. DON'T YOU EVER FORGET IT.

YOU PROMISED ME THAT YOU WOULD NEVER TELL ANYONE THAT YOU AND AYAKO SAW ME WASHING BLOOD OFF MY SHIRT.

IF I EVER EVEN THINK YOU HAVE, I WILL KILL YOU!

NAW, MASTA JIRO, YER SCARIN' ME! STOPPIT!

BE SCARED. DON'T WANNA DIE, DO YOU? PROMISE AGAIN YOU WON'T SAY A WORD!

N-NUH-UH, NAW, NAW, ME WON' SAY NUTHIN'.

GOOD... NOW COME, LET'S GO INTO TOWN AND GET YOU THAT KIMONO, EY?

WHY AREN'T YOU COMING? DON'T YOU WANT A KIMONO?

NOW STOP DILLY-DALLY-ING!

...

FINE. NO KIMONO FOR YOU TODAY, THEN.

WHERE'S AYAKO?

WHAT? AYAKO'S MISSIN'?!

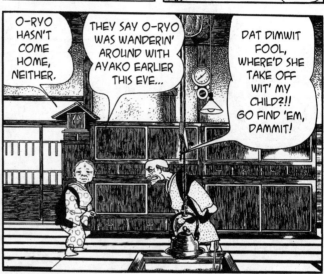
O-RYO HASN'T COME HOME, NEITHER.

THEY SAY O-RYO WAS WANDERIN' AROUND WITH AYAKO EARLIER THIS EVE...

DAT DIMWIT FOOL, WHERE'D SHE TAKE OFF WIT' MY CHILD?!! GO FIND 'EM, DAMMIT!

ANY O' YA GOTS ANY IDEAS? LIKE WHETHER SHE WERE HEADIN' TOWARDS TOWN?

...

O-RYO USUALLY TURNS UP WHEN SHE GETS HUNGRY...

THERE'S JUST ONE TIME SHE DIDN'T.

THAT WAS WHEN PA'D YELLED AT HER AND BEAT HER UP.

WHICH MEANS SOMEONE'S YELLED AT HER TODAY.

QUESTION IS, WHY'D SOMEONE INTIMIDATE O-RYO... HM?

WE'VE FOUND O-RYO 'N AYAKO.

THEY BE INSIDE DA IWAI-DEN.

COME ON OUT, O-RYO.

WHY YA BE HIDIN' IN THERE ?

YA'VE CAUSED MASTA WORRY, YA FOOL!

IF YA DON' COME OUT, WE'LL PULL YA OUT.

MISSY AYAKO, IT BE ME, GOSUKE. PLEASE COME HOME.

129

131

CHAPTER 5

HIT-BY-TRAIN

DUE TO THE
INABILITY TO
FULLY TRACK VICTIM
TADASHI ENO'S
MOVEMENTS ON
THE DAY OF HIS DEATH,
THE INVESTIGATION INTO
THE DEATH-BY-TRAIN
INCIDENT OF JUNE 17TH,
WHILE LEANING TOWARDS
A SUICIDE THEORY,
WAS MAKING LITTLE
PROGRESS.

MEANWHILE, STRIKES
PROTESTING JNR'S
MASS DISCHARGE
WERE BEING ORGANIZED
ALL ACROSS JAPAN.
ON JUNE 26TH,
THE NATIONAL RAILWAYS
WORKERS UNION
CONVENED
A CENTRAL STRIKE
COMMITTEE MEETING IN
ATAMI AND DECIDED ON
HARDLINE ACTION,
INCLUDING STRIKES.

ALL THE WHILE
THE DAY OF
RECKONING,
JULY 3RD,
CONTINUED
TO CREEP
CLOSER AND
CLOSER.

JULY 3, 1949

134

WHAT UGLINESS YOU FACE THESE DAYS, DEAR...

EVERY DAY, I WORRY AND FRET ALL DAY UNTIL YOU RETURN HOME...

...

SO MANY PETITIONS AND SAD LETTERS FROM THE FAMILIES OF THOSE BEING LET GO... I CAN'T STAND IT. IT ALMOST MAKES ME WANT TO BE LAID OFF, TOO...

SIR, THERE IS SOME-ONE HERE FROM GHQ.

DEAR ...?

LET HIM IN.

I KNOW WHY HE'S HERE.

STOMP STOMP STOMP

STOMP STOMP

STOMP

MISTER SHIMOKAWA! I ORDERED YOU TO CARRY OUT THE LAYOFFS BY JULY 3RD!

I KNOW, LIEUTENANT COLONEL CHAGNON.

THEN WHY HAVEN'T YOU?

TODAY IS A SUNDAY, SO I THOUGHT I'D DO IT ON THE 4TH.

I'M PRETTY SURE I NOTIFIED GHQ ABOUT IT...

IT DOESN'T MATTER! IF I TOLD YOU TO DO IT ON JULY 3RD, THEN YOU JUST OBEY MY ORDERS!

PLEASE CALM DOWN, LT. COLONEL.

OUR OFFICES ARE CLOSED ON SUNDAY, THERE'S NO WAY TO GET THE WORD OUT. I'D NEED THE GOVERNMENT'S ASSISTANCE IF I WERE TO FORCE...

MMMM

SHIMO-KAWA! YOU ARE INSUB-ORDINATE!

DON'T WORRY. I SHALL MAKE THE ANNOUNCE-MENT TOMOR-ROW.

THAT NEXT DAY,
ON JULY 4TH,
JNR PRESIDENT
NORIYUKI SHIMOKAWA
ANNOUNCED THE FIRING
OF 33,963 EMPLOYEES.
FOLLOWING THAT,
HE AND OTHER JNR
EXECUTIVES TOOK
REFUGE IN THE
TRANSPORTATION
ASSOCIATION CLUB,
WHERE HE APPEARED
DEEP IN THOUGHT,
BATTLING DISTRESS.
AND THEN...
JULY 5TH ARRIVED.

SIR... WHERE SHALL I TAKE YOU?

I NEED TO GO SHOPPING, SO DRIVE ME TO MITSUKO-SHI.

MITSUKOSHI IS STILL CLOSED, SIR. THEY DON'T OPEN UNTIL 9:30...

THEN TO CHIYO-DA BANK...

BACK TO MITSU-KOSHI.

I'LL ONLY BE ABOUT 5 MINUTES.

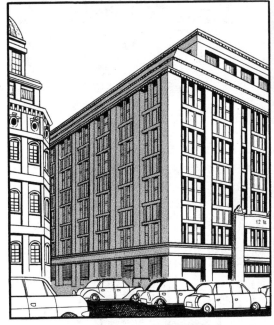

WHAT'S TAKING HIM SO LONG? IT'S BEEN 3 HOURS NOW.

IT APPEARS JNR PRESIDENT NORIYUKI SHIMOKAWA HAS GONE MISSING TODAY. AT THIS PRESENT TIME OF 5PM, HIS WHEREABOUTS ARE STILL NOT...

HELLO? THIS IS PRESIDENT SHIMO-KAWA'S DRIVER!

THE JNR PRESIDENT IS MIA! ACCORDING TO HIS DRIVER'S STATEMENT, HE ENTERED MITSU-KOSHI DEPARTMENT STORE AND HAS NOT EMERGED SINCE.

SUZUKI, YOU COMB THROUGH MITSUKOSHI FROM TOP TO BOTTOM. NAKAMURA, YOU HIT UP ANY PLACES THE PRESIDENT FREQUENTS, ONE BY ONE!

DEPENDING ON OUR FINDINGS, WE MAY HAVE TO SET UP A SPECIAL IN-VESTIGATIONS HQ...

INSPECTOR, I'M WONDERING IF PERHAPS SOME LEFT-WING FACTION HAS ABDUCTED HIM.

THAT YOUR GUT, OR...

YEAH... JUST INSTINCT.

ACTUALLY, I DID HAVE THE SAME HUNCH...

BUT IF HE SHOWS UP SAFE AND SOUND, WE'LL BE DIS-GRACED.

PUT ME THROUGH TO THE SHIMOKAWA RESIDENCE... YEAH, IT'S ME. HOW'S HIS FAMILY DOING? WELL, WE STILL DON'T HAVE MUCH TO GO ON, HERE, EITHER.

141

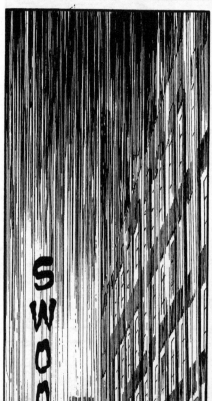

AT 2:30AM ON JULY 6TH, THE DISMEMBERED HIT-BY-TRAIN CORPSE DISCOVERED ON THE TRACKS OF THE JOBAN LINE IN THE VICINITY OF AYASE WAS CONFIRMED AS THAT OF PRESIDENT SHIMOKAWA. BY 6AM, THE METROPOLITAN POLICE DEPARTMENT LAUNCHED ITS OFFICIAL CRIME SCENE INSPECTION, AND A LARGE INVESTIGATORY GROUP OF CLOSE TO 60 PEOPLE, WHICH INCLUDED CSI, DETECTIVES, AND PUBLIC PROSECUTORS, RUSHED TO THE SCENE.

NON-AUTHOR-IZED PERSONS, PLEASE MOVE ASIDE!!

MEM-BERS OF THE PRESS, STEP BACK!

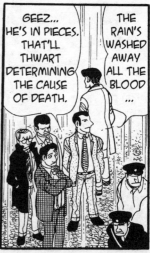

GEEZ... HE'S IN PIECES, THAT'LL THWART DETERMINING THE CAUSE OF DEATH.

THE RAIN'S WASHED AWAY ALL THE BLOOD ...

144

I SUSPECT QUITE A FEW TRAINS RAN OVER THE BODY, INSPECTOR...

YEAH...

INSPECTOR, LET'S LEAVE THIS IN OUR COLLEAGUES' HANDS AND GO LOOK AT THE AUTOPSY RESULTS AT TOKYO U.

HOLD ON.

THERE'S SOMETHING ABOUT THIS.

I VAGUELY REMEMBER HEARING ABOUT A SIMILAR CASE, ANOTHER DEATH-BY-TRAIN INCIDENT.

DISMEMBERED CORPSE... RAIN... BLOODSTAINS WASHED AWAY... OVERNIGHT...

HMM... WAS IT RECENTLY...?

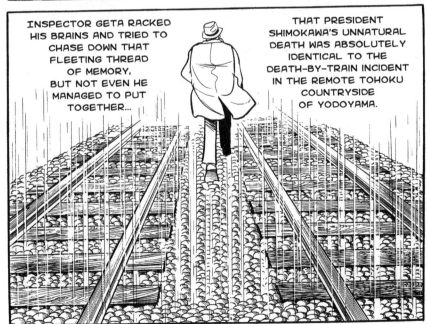

INSPECTOR GETA RACKED HIS BRAINS AND TRIED TO CHASE DOWN THAT FLEETING THREAD OF MEMORY, BUT NOT EVEN HE MANAGED TO PUT TOGETHER...

THAT PRESIDENT SHIMOKAWA'S UNNATURAL DEATH WAS ABSOLUTELY IDENTICAL TO THE DEATH-BY-TRAIN INCIDENT IN THE REMOTE TOHOKU COUNTRYSIDE OF YODOYAMA.

JULY 7, 1949

THE METROPOLITAN POLICE ESTABLISHED A SPECIAL INVESTIGATION HQ WITHIN CRIMINAL INVESTIGATIONS, SECTION 1, TO LOOK INTO JNR PRESIDENT SHIMOKAWA'S DEATH, AND CONVENED A GRAND COUNCIL OF 43 FROM THE REGIONAL PROSECUTOR'S OFFICE, THE DETECTIVE DIVISION, AND TOKYO UNIVERSITY'S COURSE IN FORENSIC MEDICINE. THEY DETERMINED TO INVESTIGATE BOTH ANGLES, SUICIDE AND HOMICIDE, AND ASSIGNED THE FOLLOWING PARTICULAR TASKS:

1. A SQUAD TO LOOK INTO THE PRESIDENT'S PERSONAL RELATIONSHIPS.
2. A SQUAD TO SEARCH MITSUKOSHI DEPARTMENT STORE, WHERE THE PRESIDENT WAS LAST SEEN.
3. A SQUAD TO FOCUS ON THE SITE OF BODY DISCOVERY.
4. INTELLIGENCE GATHERING.
5. INVESTIGATION INTO POSSIBLE IDEOLOGICAL MOTIVES (BY SECTION 2).

SECTION 1 CHIEF EZAKI WAS NAMED OVERALL TEAM COMMANDER, AND INSPECTOR GETA WAS PUT IN CHARGE OF INVESTIGATING THE SITE, THOUGHT TO BE THE CORE OF THE CASE...

147

EIGHT WITNESSES CLAIM TO HAVE SEEN SHIMOKAWA NEAR THE SCENE, EARLIER THAT EVENING.

GOOD. GET THEIR ADDRESSES SO WE CAN QUESTION THEM MORE THOROUGHLY.

UH-HUH... I SEE.

INSPECTOR, YOU HAVE A LONG-DISTANCE CALL FROM YODOYAMA.

YODO-YAMA? I WONDER WHY.

YES, HELLO...?

THE PREFECTURAL POLICE? GO AHEAD...

GETA? IT'S ME.

IS THAT YOU, MISTER TANUMA?!

MY WORD... I'M SO SORRY TO HAVE BEEN OUT OF TOUCH...

YEAH, I'M STILL HANGING IN THERE.

YES, MY WIFE AND SON ARE BOTH WELL, THANK YOU...

MAN... IT'S HARD TO BELIEVE IT'S BEEN 10 YEARS, SINCE YOU SO KINDLY TOOK ME UNDER YOUR WING...

DON'T MENTION IT.

WHAT? YOU'LL BE COMING TO TOKYO TOMORROW EVENING?

WELL, I WOULD LIKE NOTHING BETTER THAN TO SEE YOU!

I DO KNOW YOU'RE UP TO YOUR NECK IN THAT SHIMOKAWA CASE.

WHAT TIME DO YOU ARRIVE? ...THE 4:16? I'LL MEET YOU AT TOKYO STATION, AT THE FARE GATE...

OLD-TIMER, USED TO WORK HERE.

EVER HEAR OF AN INSPECTOR TANUMA?

DID HE GET TRANSFERRED FOR CRITICIZING THE GOVERNMENT DURING THE WAR?

THAT'S RIGHT. HE WAS MY BOSS...

IT WASN'T POLITICAL CRITICISM. HE MERELY COMPLAINED ABOUT THE MILITARY POLICE'S INTERFERENCE IN A CERTAIN INCIDENT'S INVESTIGATION.

I TIP MY HAT TO THAT MAN'S PLUCK.

INSPECTOR, YOU HAVE A VISITOR.

HANAO!

YOUR LUNCH...

SHE'S WAITING OUTSIDE. SHE DIDN'T WANNA COME IN...

SHE ALSO SAID NOT TO COME DOWNSTAIRS 'CUZ YOU'RE BUSY.

I SEE... SHE OUGHT TO JUST BOLDLY STROLL ON IN.

THANKS... TELL MA I CAN'T GO HOME TONIGHT, EITHER.

YOU CAME HERE ALL BY YOURSELF?! I'M SO PROUD OF YOU. WHERE'S MA?

...

SO WHEN?

HMM. I'LL BE HOME SUNDAY TO PLAY WITH YOU.

150

CHAPTER 6

BRANDED

152

MISTER TENGE, I PRESUME?

I AM FROM THE PREFECTURAL POLICE.

YOU HAVE A DAUGHTER, MISS NAOKO, YES?

AYE, THIS GIRLIE'S BIG SIS.

IS MY NAOKO IN SOME KINDA TROUBLE?

WE JUST HAD SOME QUESTIONS ABOUT HER.

WHERE DOES SHE WORK?

I SEE, SO SHE'S A DOMESTIC HELPER?

ABOUT HER FRIENDS AND ACQUAINTANCES...

AYAKO! EY, AYAKO! DON' GO TOO FAR, YA HEAR?

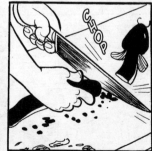

CHOP

AWW, THAT'S BLOOD!

OY, SORRY, MISS.

WAAH!

ACTUALLY, THERE'S THIS MAN MISS NAOKO WAS ENAMORED WITH... HIS NAME IS TADASHI ENO, AND HE SUFFERED AN UNNATURAL DEATH ON JUNE 17TH...

YOU MAY HAVE READ THIS IN THE PAPERS, BUT MR. ENO WAS HEAD OF DPP'S YODOYAMA CHAPTER, AND ON THE DAY OF HIS DEATH, HE HAD GONE TO TOKYO TO DELIVER FUNDS. MISS NAOKO HAD SEEN HIM OFF THE PREVIOUS DAY.

YER SAYIN' MY NAOKO HAD A THING FER A RED?

ACTUALLY, SHE HERSELF IS ALSO A DPP MEMBER. THE YODOYAMA CHAPTER'S EDUCATION AND PUBLICITY DIVISION CHIEF.

MY NAOKO'S A RED?

DAT'S ENUF WIT' YER NONSENSE!

ER... M'APOLOGIES... SORRY... T'VE YELLED AT YA...

I JUST CAN' BELIEVE... MY NAOKO'D...

YA REALLY CAN' JUDGE A SOUL BY THEIR LOOKS, EY.

I...BEEN BE-TRAYED BY MY NAOKO...

YA SEE, MY NAOKO'S HONEST 'N CHEERY JUST LIKE HER MA, A MOST PROPER GIRL.

SHE... MUST'VE BEEN SEDUCED 'N WAYLAID ...

WE'D LIKE TO ASK MISS NAOKO WHERE SHE WAS THE NIGHT OF THE INCIDENT, AND IF SHE KNOWS ANYTHING ELSE ABOUT MR. ENO.

SHE WOULD BE MAKING A VOLUN-TARY REPORT AS A REFERENCE ONLY... THAT'S ALL.

PLEASE DON'T FEAR, IT'S NOT AN ARREST.

AYE.

JIRO BRO WAS DOING
LAUNDRY IN DA
COOKING ROOM.
O-RYO SAID SHE'D
DO IT FOR 'IM.

'N THERE WAS BLOOD ON HIS SHIRT.
'N THEN BRO-BRO TOLD O-RYO
NOT TO TELL ANYONE 'BOUT IT...
THAT IF SHE DIDN'T TELL,
HE'D BUY HER A K'MONO...

SO YOUR BIG
BROTHER WAS
WASHING A BLOODY
SHIRT IN THE MIDDLE
OF THE NIGHT?

158

AND JIRO IS MISS NAOKO'S ...?

H-HER SECOND OLDEST BROTHER ...

LITTLE GIRL, DO YOU REMEMBER WHEN THAT WAS? HOW MANY DAYS AGO?

...?

PLEASE TRY TO REMEMBER. I'LL BUY YOU SOME SWEETS! THINK REAL HARD. WHEN WAS IT?

WAAAH

OH, DEAR.

ALL BOW! ALL BOW!

I'D LIKE TO PAY YOU A VISIT IN THE NEXT DAY OR SO AND MEET JIRO, ASK HIM SOME QUESTIONS.

A-ALL RIGHT ...

EACH 'N EV'RY ONE O' 'EM... HOW DARE THEY...! SHAMELESS BRATS...

FEH!

YA IN-GRATE!!

YA TRAI-TOR!!

TRAMPLIN' ALLS O'ER TH' KINDNESS O' YER PARENTS WHO'D RAISED YA...

BUT PA! THE DPP IS...

SHADDUP!

YA MENTION THEIR NAME AH-SO-CASUAL. DO YA KNOW HOW MUCH DIRT YA'VE SMEARED ON MY FACE?!

PA ...

REFORM THIS... LEFT-WING DAT...

THEY BEEN TAKIN' MY LAND FROM ME, 'N THREATENIN' ME WIT' 'EM UNION THINGS...

THEY BE THICK-HEADED RUFFIANS, TRYIN' T'STEAL ALLS MY PRO-PERTY!

NAOKO, LET ME ASK PA TO RECON- SIDER ...

I-IT'S ALL RIGHT. I DON'T WANT TO...

CAUSE ANYONE ELSE TROUBLE!

THEY SAYS SHE'S DPP.

OH, MY... I DIDN' KNOW...

SHE BE SUMMONED BY DA COPS.

MUR MUR

CAN' TELL 'EM BY LOOKIN'.

SUMMON O-RYO 'N JIRO NEXT!

WHERE JIRO BE, EY?

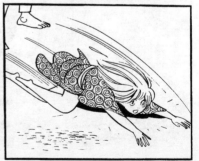

163

164

165

HA HA HA... HO HO HO HO

HA HA HA HA...

IF YOU'RE GOING TO KEEP NOSILY PRESSING THE MATTER, I WOULDN'T LET ME ANSWER UNLESS WE'RE IN PRIVATE.

OR ELSE I'LL END UP HURTING YOU, PA, HEH HEH HEH...

WH-WHAT?!! WHATS YA TALKIN' 'BOUT?

JIRO!!

QUIT LAUGHIN' LIKE A LUNATIC!!

YOU BETTER STOP ASKING SUCH BOORISH QUESTIONS, PA.

WHAT?!

I ASK YOU TO CLEAR THE ROOM. THIS HEARING SHOULD ONLY INCLUDE YOU, ME, ICHIRO, AND O-RYO...

A SECRET TRIAL, JUST THE FOUR OF US.

I DO BELIEVE THERE IS PRECEDENCE FOR SUCH WISHES OF THE ACCUSED TO BE GRANTED, UNDER THESE CUSTOMS.

ALLS O' YA, GET OUT! 'N STAY BACK 60 FEET, YA HEAR?

NOW TALK, TH' WHOLE O' IT.

ON THE NIGHT OF JUNE 17TH, O-RYO SUDDENLY MADE ADVANCES AT ME.

YEAH, I BELIEVE AROUND 10PM...

EH? WHAT SHE DO?

NOW, HERE I'VE GOT TO STAY CALM AND GIVE THEM MY ALIBI FOR THAT NIGHT, THAT I'VE BEEN HONING THIS PAST WEEK. FORTUNATELY SHE'S A HALF-WITTED GIRL, SO THERE'S NO FEAR OF ANY HOLES CROPPING UP...

THAT DAY... YOU REMEMBER, PA, DON'T YOU? WE PLAYED GO TOGETHER AND THEN I WENT TO MY ROOM TO NAP.

AROUND 10PM...

167

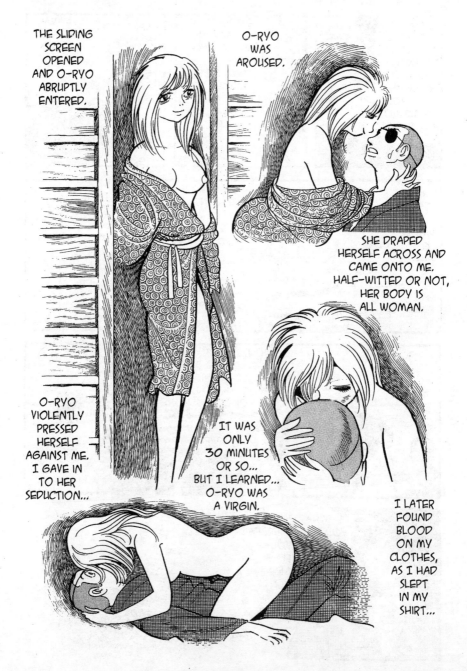

THE SLIDING SCREEN OPENED AND O-RYO ABRUPTLY ENTERED.

O-RYO WAS AROUSED.

SHE DRAPED HERSELF ACROSS AND CAME ONTO ME. HALF-WITTED OR NOT, HER BODY IS ALL WOMAN.

O-RYO VIOLENTLY PRESSED HERSELF AGAINST ME. I GAVE IN TO HER SEDUCTION...

IT WAS ONLY 30 MINUTES OR SO... BUT I LEARNED... O-RYO WAS A VIRGIN.

I LATER FOUND BLOOD ON MY CLOTHES, AS I HAD SLEPT IN MY SHIRT...

...

WHY'JA NOT SAY SO SOONER?!!

WHY DO I HAVE TO TELL ANYONE THAT I SLEPT WITH THAT GIRL?

BESIDES WHICH... O-RYO...

LEARNED ABOUT IT FROM SEEING YOU SLEEPING WITH SIS-IN-LAW IN THE STOREHOUSE SEVERAL TIMES!

JIRO!!

H-HOW DARE YA...

I'M SORRY, BIG BROTHER, TO HAVE BROUGHT THIS UP HERE AND NOW. BUT THE MORE I GET POKED, THE MORE I MIGHT END UP AIRING ALL OF THIS FAMILY'S DIRTY LAUNDRY.

EVEN IF THERE ARE POLICE ...AND OTHERS ...PRESENT...

O-RYO!!

AYE...?

169

170

HO HO HO HO HO HO, HA HA HA HA!! MWA-HA HA HA HA!

GOTCHA, BIG BRO! PA!

I WIN, I'M SAFE! YOU'VE NO LEG TO STAND ON AGAINST ME.

TAKE O-RYO AWAY.

HEY, IT'S ALL OVER.

THERE WAS NOTHING TO IT?

NOPE, NOTHING, ESPECIALLY NOT FOR CHILDREN'S EARS.

BIG BRO, WHAT'JA DO WITH THAT BLOODY SHIRT? DID'JA TOSS IT?

I DID!

WHERE?

171

WHAT DOES IT MATTER, WHERE I TOSSED IT?!

I TOLD YOU, THIS IS NOT CHILDREN'S BUSINESS!

ARE YOU SURE ABOUT THAT? WHAT IF THE POLICE FIND THAT SHIRT AND CHECK THE BLOOD TYPE? I BET IT'LL MATCH...

QUIET!

CURSE THAT SHIRO... NEED TO BE ON MY GUARD AROUND HIM. HE'S WAY TOO UPRIGHT AND INTELLIGENT FOR A TENGE.

HE MIGHT BE THE FOE I NEED TO BE THE MOST CAREFUL ABOUT.

174

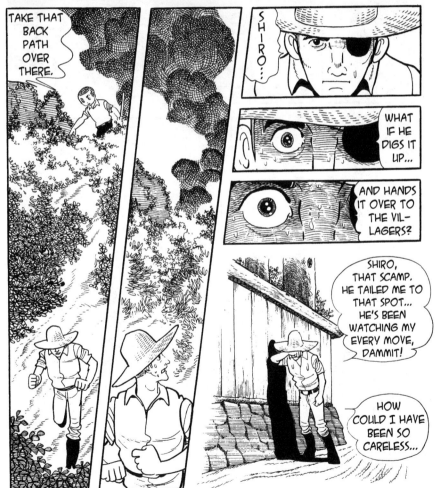

175

177

CHAPTER 7

MIMICRY

JULY 8, 1949

IT WAS A SCORCHING HOT DAY IN TOKYO.

THE METROPOLITAN POLICE'S
SPECIAL INVESTIGATION HQ RESUMED ITS
MULTI-PRONGED INQUIRY EARLY THAT MORNING.
THE PRESS MADE PRESIDENT SHIMOKAWA'S
UNNATURAL DEATH THEIR FRONT-PAGE STORY,
AND A FIERCE SCOOPS BATTLE ENSUED.
MAINICHI SHIMBUN PUT WEIGHT ON THE SUICIDE THEORY
IN AN ARTICLE, WHILE *ASAHI* AND OTHER PAPERS
CLUNG TO THE HOMICIDE ANGLE.
CANVASSING OF THE SCENE ENVIRONS AND THE
SEARCH OF MITSUKOSHI DEPARTMENT STORE YIELDED
FEW USEFUL CLUES, FURTHER DEEPENING
THE MYSTERY SURROUNDING THE CASE.

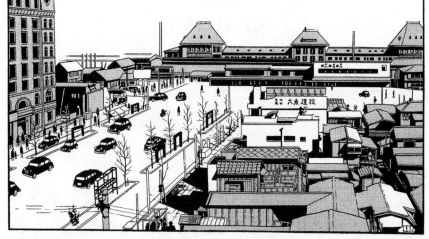

THE TRAIN NOW ARRIVING ON TRACK 18 IS THE 16:16...

YO, GETA...

MISTER TANUMA!!

WELCOME... YOU MUST BE TIRED.

MR. TANUMA... YOU HAVEN'T CHANGED A BIT THESE 10 YEARS.

GETA, YA MUST BE SO BUSY. ARE YA SURE YA'VE GOT THE TIME?

I MUST INSIST THAT YOU SPEND THE NIGHT AT MY PLACE. IT'S NOT THAT SPACIOUS, BUT MY WIFE AND SON ARE EAGERLY AWAITING YOU...

WELL, I SURE AM GRATEFUL, BUT I'D LIKE T'HEAD BACK AS SOON AS I'VE CONCLUDED MY BUSINESS.

WHOA NOW... SO WHAT DID BRING YOU TO TOKYO, SIR?

I WANTED T'ASK YA SOMETHING, GETA.

HUH? ME?

ABOUT THE SHIMO-KAWA INCIDENT...

183

MA, OUR MUCH-EXPECTED GUEST IS HERE.

MA'AM, IT'S ME, TA-NUMA.

OH!

WEL-COME!

PLEASE, COME IN!

PLEASE, AS YA WERE. I'LL BE TAKING A TRAIN BACK THIS EV'N-ING.

I'VE GOT SOME SUPER-COLD BEER!

THAT'D BE GREAT.

HEY, MAMA, YOU KNOW THAT MAN?

YES, I OWE HIM A DEBT OF GRATITUDE, FROM WHEN I WAS YOUNGER.

MISTER TANUMA!!

THAT'S THE INQUIRY REPORT FER THE JUNE 17TH DEATH-BY-TRAIN INCIDENT IN MY JURISDICTION.

WHAT A SHOCKER... THIS IS TOTALLY IDENTICAL TO THE SHIMOKAWA CASE!

AIN'T IT? DISMEMBERED CORPSE, RAIN, BLOODSTAINS WASHED AWAY, PLUS EYEWITNESS ACCOUNTS...

NOW I REMEMBER. I'D READ ABOUT THIS CASE IN THE PAPERS.

SOMETHING TRIGGERED MY MEMORY AS I WAS INSPECTING MY CRIME SCENE... THE SIMILARITIES.

AND YOUR TAKE? WAS IT SUICIDE, OR MURDER?

186

...

PLEASE, MA'AM, DON'T CONCERN YERSELF OVER ME.

WE DON'T HAVE MUCH, BUT PLEASE ENJOY YOUR TIME HERE.

SORRY, MA, WE'RE DISCUSSING A SERIOUS MATTER.

THERE'S ONE FISHY CHAP, A LANDOWNER'S SON BY THE NAME OF JIRO TENGE...

OH?

BUT THE WITNESSES ARE A 4-YEAR-OLD GIRL 'N A SLOW-WITTED WOMAN.

HE WAS SEEN WASHING A BLOODSTAINED SHIRT LATE THAT NIGHT.

I HAD A CHANCE T'SPEAK WITH THE FELLA, BUT HE CLAIMS THE BLOOD IS FROM AN ENTIRELY UNRELATED EVENT.

YET HIS ALIBI IS INCOMPLETE, PLUS I SUSPECT HIS FAMILY IS COVERING FER HIM...

THE SHIRT'S WHEREABOUTS 'N THE SOURCE OF BLOOD ARE UNKNOWN.

COULD HE PERHAPS BE INNOCENT?

I JUST CAN'T LET IT GO.

IT ALSO BOTHERS ME THAT THIS JIRO CHAP'S LITTLE SISTER WAS THE LOVER OF THE DECEASED, ENO...

IN ANY CASE, WHAT'S PECULIAR IS THE SIMILARITY BETWEEN THE TWO INCIDENTS!

THAT'S RIGHT... WHICH IS WHY I WANTED YA T'KNOW ABOUT IT.

MR. TANUMA, MAY I OFFER YOU MY OPINION?

THE YODOYAMA CASE WAS A TEMPLATE FOR THE SHIMOKAWA CASE...

MM-HMM.

AND ONCE YODOYAMA HAPPENED... THE SHIMOKAWA CASE...

HAPPENED AS A MATTER OF COURSE!

191

A HALF-WIT AND A 4-YEAR-OLD GIRL...

THE FOUR YEAR OLD WILL EVENTUALLY GROW UP, AND THE SLOW GIRL MAY YET GAIN HER WITS.

IT'S JUST WORRISOME.

ONE OF THEM IS MY YOUNGEST SISTER...

MAKE THEIR DEATHS LOOK LIKE ACCIDENTS.

HOW BRUTAL.

I THOUGHT YOU WERE DONE WITH PANGS OF CONSCIENCE?

JUST DON'T EVER DITCH ME.

NOTE: "HELL FLOWER" IS LYCORIS RADIATA, OR THE RED SPIDER LILY. WHILE IT IS POISONOUS, IT DOES NOT ACTUALLY CAUSE CLOTTING OR BLEEDING DISORDERS.

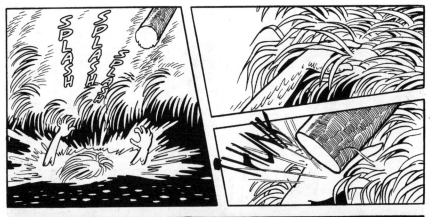

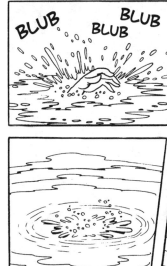

200

"SOB SOB"
"SOB"

WAAH

ICHI-RO!!

I KNOW HOW YOU FEEL, PA, BUT THIS IS THE ONLY SOLUTION.

YA FIGURES YA CAN DO SUCH A CRUEL DEED 'CUZ SHE AIN' YER ISSUE?!

THAT AIN'T IT!

WITH O-RYO DYING THE WAY SHE DID, THE COPS WILL BE ALL OVER AYAKO!

WHAT COULDS A 4 YEAR-OLD TELL 'EM?! YER JUMPIN' TH' GUN!

PA, PUT YOURSELF IN MY SHOES, FOR ONCE.

THANKS TO JIRO, WE'VE GOTTEN SWEPT UP IN THIS STUPID CASE... DON'T YOU CARE WHAT RUMORS MIGHT SPREAD?

WE TENGES ARE NOT UNKNOWN IN THESE PARTS. IF WE FALL TO ILL REPUTE, WHAT OF MY STANDING AS SUCCEEDING HEIR?

WE'LL PUT AYAKO AWAY UNTIL THE COPS STOP SNIFFING AROUND!

ONLY UNTIL THE HUBBUB DIES DOWN. PLEASE UNDERSTAND.

WHATS WE GONNA TELL 'EM POLICE ...?

MAYBE THAT SHE'S BEDRIDDEN AND CAN'T HAVE VISITORS?

WHAT?! THE DIM-WITTED GIRL IS DEAD?

SO VERY TRAGIC, BUT HER BODY WAS FOUND FLOATING IN THE SWAMP.

WAS ANYONE WITH HER? WE WERE GIVEN TO UNDERSTAND THAT THE CHILD AYAKO IS ALWAYS AT HER SIDE.

AYAKO'S CAUGHT A TERRIBLE COLD...

AND IS ASLEEP IN THE BACK. SHE'S RUN A HIGH FEVER AND MUSTN'T BE DISTURBED.

CAN WE DISTURB HER JUST A SEC?

NOT EVEN IF YOU'RE THE POLICE, I CANNOT ALLOW IT!

CHAPTER 8

THE CELLAR

O-RYO, WHY YA BE DEAD...

WHOEVER PUSH YA IN DA WATER?

I SWEARS T'FIND 'EM 'N AVENGE YA, EY...

210

...

SHOZA SHOZA

EV'RYONE HERE...?

THE ONLY ONE MISSING IS NAOKO.

AS YA'LL KNOWS, THERE BE A RUMOR O-RYO WAS KILLED BY SOMEBODY. AYAKO'S ACTIN' SCARED 'N HIDIN' FROM SOMEBODY... SHE KNOWS SOMETHIN' BUT SHE BE TOO SCARED T'TALK. HOWEV'R...

WHATEV'R IT BE, I BETCHA IT BE SOMETHIN' DAT SHALL STAIN THE TENGE CLAN'S NAME, IF SHE WERE T'EVER TALK.

THUS...

I CALLED THIS MEET T'DECIDE WHAT T'DO 'BOUT HER.

SO WHAT IS IT, EXACTLY?

THIS THING AYAKO KNOWS...

MM... I–IF WE KNEW, YA ALL WOULDN' BE HERE.

JUST, TH' POLICE BEEN SNOOPIN' AROUND THESE PAST FEW DAYS...

POLICE COMIN' BY MEANS IT AIN' GOOD.

WE GOTS T'DO SOME-THIN'.

WHAT 'BOUT SENDIN' HER T'SOME RELATIONS FAR AWAY?

FOOL! WE TALKIN' 'BOUT DA POLICE HERE. SUCH ELEMEN'ARY TACTICS AIN' GONNA FOOL 'EM!

...

HMM...

OUR ONLY CHOICE IS T'HAVE HER DIE...

HAVE HER DIE?!

ICHI... YA SAYIN' YA GONNA KILL DA CHILD?

NAW... JUST TAKE HER OFF TH' BOOKS...

PRETEND SHE PASSED AWAY, 'N SEND OUT A DEATH NOTICE.

'N WHAT'RE YA GONNA DO WIT' HER? YER AIN' GONNA HAVE HER PRETEND T'BE DEAD HER WHOLE LIFE?

THAT'S RIGHT!

MOST UNFORTUNATE, BUT AYAKO MUST STAY SEQUESTERED 'TIL SHE DIES.

B-BUT ...

...THAT'S CRUEL.

OR WHAT ...

THAT CHILD WASN'T BORN UNDER LUCKY STARS... IT CAN'T BE HELPED.

WOULD YA RATHER TH' TENGE NAME GET TARNISHED?!

DO YA WANT US T'BE A HOUSE THAT FOLKS POINT AT 'N TREAT WIT' CONTEMPT, PRIEST OF NAKANOTANI?

N-N-NO, THAT'D CAUSE ME PROBLEMS, TOO.

MY TEMPLE'S STANDIN' HAS RISEN THANKS T'YER FAMILY'S PATRONAGE.

WHAT ABOUTS YA, MISTER TOSAKU?

MY SHOP DRAWS CUSTOMERS CUZ I'M A TENGE RELATION. THEY'D STOP COMIN' IN IF THERE BE TROUBLE.

EIZO FROM HIGASHI-MURA?

I AIN' WANT DA TENGE CLAN PRODUCIN' NO CRIMINALS.

FOOL, WHO SAID ANYTHIN' 'BOUT PRODUCIN' CRIMINALS?

WHAT 'BOUTS YA, MISSUS KURUWA?

YEAH, ME BRATS WOULD FEEL MIGHTY SHAMED.

ANY OTHER COMMENTS?

THEN LET'S PUT IT T'VOTE... EACH O' YA GOTS TWO BOWLS IN FRONT O' YA. PLACE TH' BIGGER ONE FACE DOWN IF YA AGREE, TH' SMALLER ONE IF YER AGAINST.

THIS BE JUST TOO MUCH!

ALL FER TH' FAMILY, PA!

KLOMP

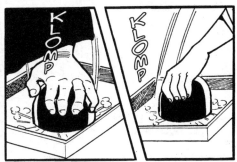

KLOMP

KLOMP

215

CONFINE INNOCENT AYAKO, ALL ALONE, FOR THE REST OF HER LIFE? NOW *THAT* IS TRULY CRIMINAL, IF YOU ASK ME.

SHIRO!

WHY ARE YA AGAINST 2!

QUIT IT WIT' YER WISECRACK COMMENTS, SHIRO!

CHANGE YER VOTE!

NO WAY.

AND MINE ISN'T THE ONLY NAY.

WHO ELSE OBJECTS?

NAOKO BIG SIS DOES!

HMPH. NAOKO AIN' PART O' THIS FAMILY NO MORE!

THAT ONLY TAKES EFFECT AFTER THIS INCIDENT IS WRAPPED UP, PA.

BEFORE THIS MEETING WAS CALLED, I HAD NAOKO BIG SIS WRITE DOWN HER OPINION. THIS IS IT.

SHE VOTES "AGAINST"!

217

THAT AIN' COUNTIN' AS A VOTE!

I'D LIKE TO SAY A FEW WORDS, IF I MAY?

AYAKO'S SEEN AND KNOWS THE PERPETRATOR WHO KILLED O-RYO.

'N THAT'S TH' PROBLEM, CAN' YA UNDERSTAND THAT?

WHOEV'R AYAKO SAW O' WHATEV'R THEY TRIED T'DO, WE CAN' HAVE THIS HOUSE DRAGGED INTO IT!!

I BELIEVE THE PERP WAS ORIGINALLY PLANNING TO KILL BOTH O-RYO AND AYAKO...

...HAD TARGETED THE TWO OF THEM ALL ALONG, FOR HAVING SEEN A CERTAIN SOMETHING.

SHUT IT, SHIRO!!

I-I AIN' FERGIVIN' YA FER THIS DISRUPTION, Y'FOOL...

THE PERP HAD COMMITTED MURDER, AND THE VICTIM'S BLOOD GOT ON HIS CLOTHES... THAT'S WHAT THE TWO WITNESSED.

BLOOD!!

A MURDER?

I PRESENT TO YOU A PIECE OF THAT SHIRT.

THIS IS THE BLOOD THEY SAW.

THE PERP TRIED TO BURY THIS SHIRT IN THE GROUND, TO HIDE IT...

STILL WORRIED, HE THEN TRIED TO BURN IT.

I DUG IT UP AND CUT OUT THIS SCRAP.

FWUP!!

THIS PAPER IS FROM JUNE 18TH... AN INCREDIBLE INCIDENT OCCURRED THE NIGHT BEFORE.

YOU MAY REMEMBER THAT SOMEONE WAS RUN OVER BY A TRAIN, BACK TOWARDS TOWN.

THEY'RE NOT SURE IF IT WAS SUICIDE OR A HOMICIDE...

RAIN STARTED FALLING THAT EVENING...

AND WENT ON 'TIL MIDNIGHT.

THE OTHER DAY, WHEN I ASKED AYAKO... SHE SAID SHE SAW THE PERSON WITH THE BLOODY CLOTHES ON A RAINY NIGHT, AROUND MIDNIGHT.

QUIET!!

I ALWAYS RECORD WHEN IT STARTS AND STOPS RAINING, IN MY DIARY. IN THE PAST 10 DAYS, THE ONLY NIGHT IT RAINED UNTIL MIDNIGHT WAS THE 17TH!

WHICH MEANS IT WAS ON THE 17TH... THE NIGHT THAT PERSON GOT RUN OVER, THAT AYAKO WITNESSED THE BLOOD!

GET OUT 'N GET LOST, SHIRO!

IF YA DON' SHUT UP, WE'LL WRAP YA IN A MAT 'N THROW YA IN DA CLOSET!!

NAW, I GOTTA SPEAK ON AYAKO'S BEHALF.

I'M GONNA LET THEM TYPE THE BLOOD. IF IT MATCHES THAT VICTIM'S...

GRR!

UNH!

HEY, YOU CAN'T TAKE THAT! NAW!

GIVE IT BACK, GIVE IT BACK!

...

JIRO... Y'...

I AIN'T GONNA ASK. JUST GO, 'N NEVER COME BACK T'THIS VILLAGE!

WE'LL CLEAN UP HERE!

FOR THAT, BROTHER, THANK YOU.

EVERYONE, LISTEN UP!

FOR THE SAKE O' OUR HOUSE NAME, MAKE SURE OUR STORIES MATCH! AYAKO'S DEAD... FROM PNEUMONIA!!

FILL IN TH' CELLAR WINDOW. USE DIRT.

THEN LAY PLASTER O'ER IT!

MAKE SURE AYAKO'S VOICE CAN'T LEAK OUT.

MA, WE NEED A FAKE FUNERAL.

GOOD, O-RYO'S FUNERARY THINGS ARE STILL AROUND.

JUST NEED T'PREPARE AN EXTRA COFFIN 'N BURY IT.

MISTER!

223

225

226

227

ACUTE PNEUMONIA?!

YOU'RE SAYING THAT FOLLOWING THE UNNATURAL DEATH OF YOUR MAID O-RYO, THE LITTLE GIRL ALSO PASSED AWAY, FROM ACUTE PNEUMONIA?

MY WORD... WHAT TERRIBLE GRIEF YOU MUST BE FEELING.

WE NEVER IMAGINED WE'D SUFFER SUCH MISFORTUNE, T'LOSE BOTH SO SUDDENLY.

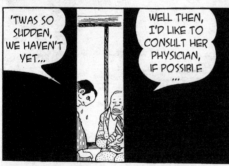

HATE TO BOTHER YOU DURING THIS TIME OF DISTRESS...

BUT DO YOU HAVE A COPY OF THE LITTLE GIRL'S DEATH CERTIFICATE?

'TWAS SO SUDDEN, WE HAVEN'T YET...

WELL THEN, I'D LIKE TO CONSULT HER PHYSICIAN, IF POSSIBLE...

THAT'D BE ME.

I'M YAMAZAKI, FROM NAKANO-MORI.

I ATTEST THAT I WAS AT HER DEATHBED.

DIRECT CAUSE O' DEATH WAS SOMETHIN' CALLED "CARDIAC BREAKDOWN."

PARDON ME, BUT YOUR CONNECTION TO MISTER TENGE...?

SURE, I'M HIS COUSIN ON MY FA-THER'S SIDE.

SO YOU ARE RE-LATED...

I DON'T KNOW WHAT TO SAY...

ALL THE NOTABLE FOLK IN THIS AREA SAY THEY ARE A TENGE!

WELL... THAT'S 'CUZ...

TH' TENGES A RIGHT OLD FAMILY THAT'S BEEN AROUND 400 YEARS. IF I MAY, WE AIN'T TH' SAME AS THOSE NOUVEAU RICHE 'N OTHER UPSTARTS YA SEE SCRABBLIN' ABOUT.

I SEE... INDEED.

THANK YOU FOR YOUR TIME.

I'D LOVE TO EVENTUALLY PAY MY RESPECTS TO MISS AYAKO'S GRAVE...

EY, THEY'RE LEAVIN'!

229

WE'D APPRECIATE IT IF MISTER JIRO COULD PRESENT HIMSELF AS SOON AFTER HE RETURNS AS POSSIBLE...

YES, I'LL LET HIM KNOW.

PHEW. THANKS SO MUCH FER PLAYIN' WITNESS...

I'M SUCH A POOR TALKER THAT IT'S EMBARRASSIN'.

THAT LEVEL O' INVESTIGATIN' AIN'T NOTHIN' T'WORRY 'BOUT.

MY WORD, WHAT A TOUGH BUNCH.

BLOOD RELATIONS COVERING FOR EACH OTHER.

THAT YOUNG MASTER, ICHIRO, HE'S QUITE A CUNNING OLD FOX, HIMSELF!

COULD THAT AYAKO CHILD REALLY BE DEAD?

I WONDER. ESPECIALLY SINCE THAT DOCTOR IS A RELATIVE, TOO.

THEY CAN COOK UP WHATEVER THEY WANT.

BUT HOW TIMES HAVE CHANGED.

5 YEARS AGO, WE COULD JUST THROW OUR WEIGHT AROUND AND FORCE IT OUT OF FOLKS...

230

AT THIS RATE, WE'RE GOING TO HAVE TO USE A BACK-DOOR APPROACH... TAKE OUR SWEET OLD TIME. FIRST, LET'S THOROUGHLY INVESTIGATE JIRO.

THIS JIRO CHARACTER IS STIFF-NECKED AND TOUGH. HE'S NOT GOING TO STICK HIS HEAD BACK OUT FOR JUST ANY LITTLE THING... YOU'RE NOT WORRIED HE MIGHT SKIP TOWN?

WHETHER HE RUNS OR HIDES, WE'LL STILL PROCEED AT OUR OWN PACE. I'VE BEEN KEEPING MYSELF FED LIKE THIS FOR 30 YEARS NOW.

BRING ME A DEAD CHICKEN AND A SHIRT.

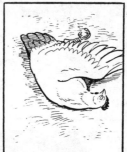

RRRIP

HEH HEH. HEH HEH HEH...

STOP IT! STUPID, STUPID BIG BRO, I HATE YOU!

I'M GONNA GO TELL THEM THE TRUTH! TELL THE POLICE EVERYTHING ABOUT US!!

233

234

CHAPTER 9

TESTIMONY

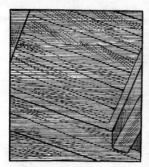

YOU MUST BE SO HUNGRY, YOU POOR THING...

KLAK
KRIIIK

SIS!

OH MY... YOU'RE ALL WET... DID YOU WEE-WEE?

I'M HUNG-WY!

HOLD YOUR HORSES, CHANGE CLOTHES FIRST...

HERE, EAT YOUR FILL.

CHOMP CHOMP
UM-GULP CHOMP

238

HUSHABYE BABY, ROCK YOURSELF TO SLEEP
HUSHABYE BABY, ROCK YOURSELF TO SLEEP

MY CUTE LITTLE BABY,
WHO WAS WATCHING YOU?
WHO WAS WATCHING YOU?

NO ONE WAS WATCHING YOU,
SO HERE COMES
SO HERE COMES...

HUSHABYE BABY,
ROCK YOURSELF TO SLEEP
HUSHABYE BABY,
ROCK YOURSELF TO SLEEP

COME, CLOSE YOUR EYES.

DON'T STARE SO AT SIS LIKE THAT.

IF YOU DON'T GO TO SLEEP, FROM THE MOUNTAINS WILL COME MONSTERS

IF YOU START CRYING, FROM THE LAND WILL COME OGRES

MY DEAR AYAKO GO TO SLEEP

GO TO SLEEP AYE, AYE, AYE

240

AYAKO ...

CALL ME "MAMA"... JUST ONCE?

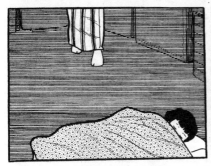

OH!

HOW'S AYAKO?

ASLEEP

FATHER, PLEASE HELP HER!!

241

I THINK IT BE A SHAME, TOO...

BUT IT CAN' BE HELPED. IT BE... ICHIRO'S DECISION ...

IF YOU KEEP HER IN SUCH A COLD PLACE, SHE'LL DIE! PLEASE LET HER OUT, FOR HEAVEN'S SAKE.

WE COULD SNEAKS HER OUT 'N PUT HER SOME-WHERE ELSE...

BUT FER ME T'CON-VINCE ICHIRO...

THAT ALL DEPENDS ON YA ...

...

BUT FATHER!! AYAKO'S... SLEEPING BELOW US!!

SHE WON' HEAR NU-THIN' ...

PLEASE DO TAKE CARE OF AYAKO... I BEG YOU...

SURE, SURE.

242

I AIN'T SCARED! N-NO SIRREE!! STUPID JERKS!

STUPID JERKS !!

...

...

OY SAW IT AWL GO DOWN FROM HEER... BUT OY CAN' AFFORD T'SHOW MESELF... TAT'S WHY OY WAITED SO WONG.

MY FWACE? HEHEH... IT'S PWITTY HOWWIBLE, EY.

ACCIDENT?

'TWAS NO ACCIDENT.

I WAS PUMMELED...

BY DA WAY... ARE YA STWILL PWANNIN' T'CONTINUE SEARCHIN' FER DA PERP DAT KIWWED ENO?

YEAH, SURE AM.

I SEE...

HEER, A FWASHWIGHT. OY'VE GOT TWO, SO OY'LL LEND YA ONE... GO HOME!

OH, 'N DON' MENTION ME T'ANYWON, OKAY?

OY'M ESCAPIN' DEEFER INTO DA FOWEST!

ESCAPING?

WHY?

246

247

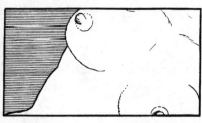

YA AIN' SO EAGER, LATELY!

I-I STILL GOTS PLENTY LOTS LEFT T'PLEASE YA, BUT YA AIN' RESPONDIN'!

B-BUT... AYAKO'S DOWN BELOW.

QUITS WORRYIN' 'BOUT HER! SHE AIN' NO INFANT!

DID DAT GOOD-FER-NUTHIN' ICHIRO SAY SOMETHIN' T'YA?

OH, SHE'S WATCHING!!

HUH?

FOOL!! SU'E, DID'JA FERGET T'BOLT TH' TRAP DOOR SHUT?!

A-AYAKO... GO BACK TO SLEEP...

GO SLEEP!!

AYAKO, LISTEN TO ME!!

DON'T LOOK!!

GO BACK DOWN!!

WAAAH!!!

SOB SOB SOB

WAAH WAAH

HOW LUDICROUS!! INTERRUPTIN' TH' BEST PART!

GAH... NOWS I'VE LOST MY DESIRE.

251

WAH!

DARN IT!!
IF IT AIN'
DAT BRAT
SHIRO!
WHY HE
BE OUT
WANDERIN'
AROUND AT
THIS HOUR
?!!

PANT
PANT
PANT
...

HEAVE
...
HEAVE
...

253

MORN-IN'

CHIEF! AT FIRST LIGHT, HE RODE HIS BICYCLE FROM HIS VILLAGE JUST TO SEE YOU...

HE WON'T SAY WHAT IT'S REGARDING!

WHO'S THAT BOY?

I'M TANUMA. AND WHO ARE YOU, YOUNG MAN?

SHIRO TENGE!

TENGE?

HM.

P-PLEASE... HAVE THIS ANA-LYZED!

FOR BLOOD TYPE!

255

I CUT OUT THAT PIECE FROM THE SHIRT JIRO BRO. WAS TRYING TO BURN THE OTHER DAY, UP IN THE MOUNTAINS!

JIRO, YOU SAID ???

AND WHEN EXACTLY WAS THIS?

THE 8TH OF THIS MONTH.

THE 8TH... THAT'S THE DAY I WENT DOWN TO TOKYO.

A DAY AFTER THAT FESTIVAL, WHEN WE MADE THE INQUIRY.

CHIEF! COULD THIS BE A CLUE FOR DESTROYING EVIDENCE?

ANALYZE THIS BLOOD. THE CLOTH IS SOILED, SO BE REAL CAREFUL!

PHEW

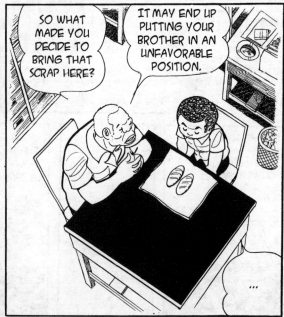

SO WHAT MADE YOU DECIDE TO BRING THAT SCRAP HERE?

IT MAY END UP PUTTING YOUR BROTHER IN AN UNFAVORABLE POSITION.

...

WE SHOULD KNOW WITHIN THE HOUR.

THANKS FOR COMING IN SO EARLY... HAVE YOU EATEN YET?

DO YOU GET ALONG WITH YOUR BIG BROTHER?

YOU KNOW, THERE'S A LOT OF THINGS I DON'T GET ABOUT YOUR FAMILY.

I'M SORRY ABOUT YOUR LITTLE SISTER.

WHEN I GAVE MY CONDOLENCES, MR. ICHIRO ONLY GAVE ME VAGUE REPLIES...

AND HIS EXPLANATIONS REGARDING THE DEATH OF THAT MAID GIRL O-RYO WAS EVEN LESS SOLID....

WHAT IN THE WORLD IS GOING ON?

SIR ...

ABOUT JIRO BIG BRO...

I THINK HE MAY'VE HAD SOMETHING TO DO WITH THAT HIT-BY-TRAIN DEATH...

OF THAT MAN ENO... WHO GOT RUN OVER ON JUNE 17TH.

WHAT EXACTLY DO YOU MEAN?

I BET THAT THAT'S ENO'S BLOOD ON THAT SHIRT!

THAT YOUR CONVICTION?

YEAH...

I DON'T HATE BIG BRO,

BUT A CRIME'S A CRIME!!

IF MY FAMILY ENDS UP LOATHING ME...

I DON'T CARE!

SHIRO! YOU'RE ONE BRAVE CHILD...

THAT WASN'T HUMAN BLOOD.

IT WAS AVIAN, PERHAPS A CHICKEN.

CHIEF! I'M DONE ANALYZING THE BLOOD.

BUT...

NO WAY!!

IT CAN'T BE TRUE...

WHY WOULD BIG BRO TRY TO BURN CHICKEN BLOOD?!!

I WAS SO SURE!!

THERE'S NO MISTAKE?

IT'S VERY EASY TO DISTINGUISH BETWEEN HUMAN AND AVIAN BLOOD.

SORRY, BUT THIS BOY IS WRONG.

SHIRO, I APPRECIATE YOUR EFFORT. IF ANYTHING COMES UP, DO LET US KNOW.

...

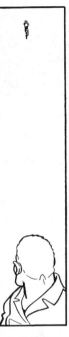

WHAT A TROUBLE-MAKER...

WHY IN THE WORLD WOULD HE BRING US CHICKEN BLOOD?

THE POINT HERE IS, EVEN HE

DOUBTS JIRO!

BRRRING

HELLO, YODOYAMA POLICE STATION...

HUH? NAKANO-MORI SUB-STATION?

CHIEF, THERE'S A CALL FOR YOU!

HUH, NAKANO-MORI...?

THEY WANT YOU AT A YAMAZAKI CLINIC IN NAKANOMORI!

HM? YES? YOU FOUND A SUSPICIOUS, DYING MAN IN A RAVINE IN OKUNO-SAWA?

AND HE'S ASKING FOR ME?

259

SIR... DO YOU RECALL EVER SEEING MY FACE BEFORE?

MAYBE NOT... WITH IT SO DEFORMED ...

LET ME JUST TELL YOU MY TALE, SINCE I DON'T HAVE LONG ...

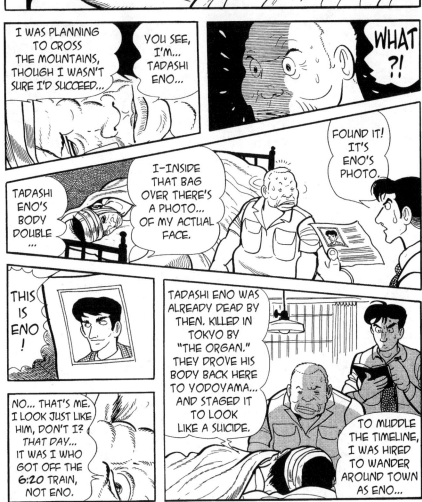

I WAS PLANNING TO CROSS THE MOUNTAINS, THOUGH I WASN'T SURE I'D SUCCEED...

YOU SEE, I'M... TADASHI ENO...

WHAT ?!

FOUND IT! IT'S ENO'S PHOTO.

TADASHI ENO'S BODY DOUBLE ...

I—INSIDE THAT BAG OVER THERE'S A PHOTO... OF MY ACTUAL FACE.

THIS IS ENO !

TADASHI ENO WAS ALREADY DEAD BY THEN, KILLED IN TOKYO BY "THE ORGAN." THEY DROVE HIS BODY BACK HERE TO YODOYAMA... AND STAGED IT TO LOOK LIKE A SUICIDE.

NO... THAT'S ME. I LOOK JUST LIKE HIM, DON'T I? THAT DAY... IT WAS I WHO GOT OFF THE 6:20 TRAIN, NOT ENO.

TO MUDDLE THE TIMELINE, I WAS HIRED TO WANDER AROUND TOWN AS ENO...

DOES THAT MEAN THAT THE FELLA WHO APPEARED AT ENO'S FACTORY THAT DAY... WAS YOU, NOT ENO?

WHO GAVE YOU YOUR ORDERS? AND WHY ALL THE THEATRICS?

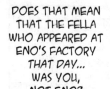

I JUST DID AS I WAS TOLD... I HAVE ABSOLUTELY NO CLUE ABOUT THEIR MOTIVES.

DUNNO THE NAME OF THE MAN WHO GAVE MY ORDERS, NOR WHO THE BOSS IS.

WHAT IS THIS "ORGAN"?!

WHERE'S THIS "ORGAN" THAT KILLED TADASHI ENO LOCATED?

HANG IN THERE!! HEY! C'MON, MAN!!

I DUNNO... DUNNO ANYTHING... AT ALL.

ONLY THE NAME OF THE MAN WHO PLACED ENO'S CORPSE ON THE TRACKS...

WHO?!

JIRO... T-TENGE...

HM!

WHEN THE JOB WAS OVER... THE "ORGAN" THUGS TRIED TO KILL ME, THEN WENT TO WORK ON MY FACE SO NO ONE WOULD EVER RECOGNIZE ME.

BUT I MANAGED TO BREAK FREE... AND MADE A RUN FOR IT... BUT THEY CAUGHT UP AND TRIED TO FINISH ME OFF ...

THAT'S GOOD ENOUGH.

NOW, I NEED YOU TO SIGN THIS.

YOUR WITNESS STATEMENT.

SIR... D-DO YOU KNOW... A KID NAMED SHIRO TENGE...?

HM?

PERHAPS.

MIGHTY IMPRESSIVE KID...

HE INSPIRED ME TO TALK, TO TELL YOU EVERY- THING, WHEN...

SLUMP

GET ME A WARRANT FOR JIRO TENGE'S ARREST!

I'LL TAKE ANY BLAME!

SIGN IT!!

SHOOT.

CHAPTER 10

THE LIVING CORPSE

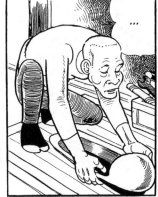

268

THE REMODELING OF THE CELLAR GAVE EVEN AYAKO'S YOUNG MIND A MOUNTING SENSE OF FOREBODING. LITTLE DID SHE REALIZE IT HAD BEEN TRANSFORMED INTO AN UNDERGROUND PRISON, A SECRET ROOM THAT WAS TANTAMOUNT TO HER GRAVE. YET THE NOW-EMPTY ROOM, WITH WARDROBES AND CHESTS REMOVED, DID SMELL OF DEATH AND FRIGHTENED HER TERRIBLY.

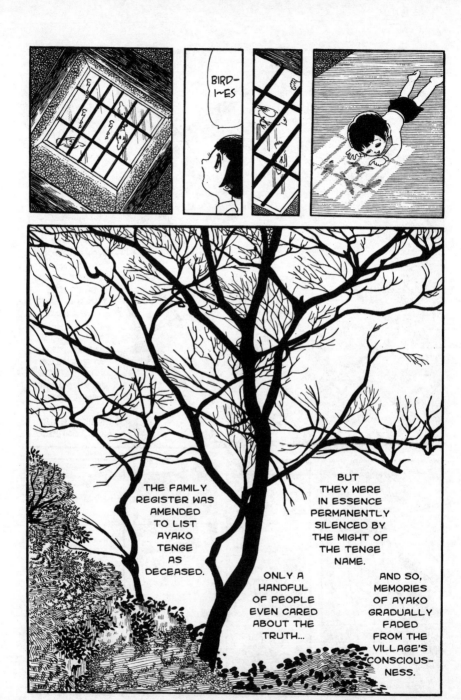

BIRD-
I~ES

THE FAMILY
REGISTER WAS
AMENDED
TO LIST
AYAKO
TENGE
AS
DECEASED.

ONLY A
HANDFUL
OF PEOPLE
EVEN CARED
ABOUT THE
TRUTH...

BUT
THEY WERE
IN ESSENCE
PERMANENTLY
SILENCED BY
THE MIGHT OF
THE TENGE
NAME.

AND SO,
MEMORIES
OF AYAKO
GRADUALLY
FADED
FROM THE
VILLAGE'S
CONSCIOUS-
NESS.

AFTER THE CHICKEN BLOOD INCIDENT, SHIRO SEEMED TO UNDERGO A REVERSAL, BECOMING MEEK AND OBEDIENT, ESPECIALLY TOWARDS ICHIRO.

JIRO VANISHED WITHOUT A TRACE ...

LEAVING INSPECTOR TANUMA FUMING, ARREST WARRANT CLENCHED IN FIST.

NAOKO ...

...HAVING BEEN BRANDED A RED AGENT BY HER FATHER, LEFT THE TENGE FAMILY FOLD, PRACTICALLY DISOWNED.

AND THE REINS OF THE TENGE FAMILY, BOTH IN NAME AND IN FACT, PASSED INTO THE HANDS OF ICHIRO.

273

WHEN I WAS YOUNG,
WE BE TH' BIGGEST LANDOWNER
'MONGST THE 14 VILLAGES!
OUR TENANT FARMERS WORKED ALL O'
TH' LAND AROUND THESE PARTS,
'N WHEN I'D DROP BY, THEY'D GREETS
ME WIT' RESPECTFUL BOWS...
NOW, SINCE TH' WAR, THEY...
THEY ALL'VE STRIPPED ME BARE
'N LEFT... DAMMIT!

275

IT WAS JULY 15, 1949, 10 DAYS AFTER THE SHIMOKAWA INCIDENT.

AT THE JNR MITAKA STATION, AN UNMANNED TRAIN MALFUNCTIONED AND JUMPED ITS TRACKS INTO A NEARBY ROAD, KILLING 10 AND WOUNDING 14.

DETERMINED A CONSPIRACY OF THE JAPAN COMMUNIST PARTY (JCP), MANY OF ITS MEMBERS IN THE RAILWAY UNION WERE ARRESTED.

FURTHERMORE, ON AUGUST 16TH, ANOTHER TRAIN DERAILED AND OVERTURNED ON THE TOHOKU MAIN LINE BETWEEN MATSUKAWA AND KANAYAGAWA, RESULTING IN THE DEATHS OF 3 CREW MEMBERS. THE AUTHORITIES BLAMED THE JCP AND INDICTED 20 UNION MEMBERS OF JNR AND TOSHIBA. THE GOVERNMENT USED THESE INCIDENTS AS AN EXCUSE TO FIERCELY INCREASE THEIR SUPPRESSION OF LEFTISTS.

THE SKY-LIGHT, THE ONLY TIE AYAKO HAD TO THE OUTSIDE...

SOME DAYS, IT'D SHOW RED LEAF UPON LEAF

SOME DAYS, A CLEAR BLUE SKY ...

ON YET OTHER DAYS, RAIN-DROPS BEAT A MONO-TONOUS RHYTHM.

AND DAY BY DAY, IT GOT COLDER AND COLDER.

EITHER WAY, ANY AND ALL NEWS OF THE WORLD HAD STOPPED REACHING AYAKO'S EARS.

MORNING, AYAKO... ARE YOU COLD?

IS THE BRAZIER I GAVE YOU LAST NIGHT STILL BURNING?

I BROUGHT YOU SOMETHING SPECIAL THIS MORNING, YOUR FAVORITE!

I KNOW, MOCHI!

THAT'S RIGHT. HOW'D YOU KNOW?

I HEARD FAINT THUMPING SOUNDS SINCE EARLY.

THE PESTLE! I KNEW RIGHT AWAY.

I SEE... NOW EAT THEM WHILE THEY'RE STILL WARM.

GONNA BE NEW YEAR'S SOON, RIGHT?

YES. TODAY IS DECEMBER 30TH, SO DAY AFTER TOMORROW IS NEW YEAR'S DAY.

SIS, YOU SAID YOU'LL LET ME OUT WHEN NEW YEAR'S CAME.

YES... THAT'S WHAT PAPA PROMISED.

PAPA'S ALWAYS SAYING "MY POOR AYAKO"...

THAT AT LEAST ON NEW YEAR'S, HE WANTS TO SNEAK YOU OUT INTO THE YARD, ALL DRESSED UP...

279

BUT ONLY FOR ONE DAY, 'CUZ WE DON'T WANT BRO TO FIND OUT...

PAPA'LL OPEN THE CELLAR DOOR.

WHAT ABOUT JIRO BRO AND NAOKO?

WE DON'T KNOW WHERE THEY ARE...

IT'S REAL LONELY IN THE HOUSE RIGHT NOW. IT'S JUST ICHIRO BRO AND SHIRO BRO.

THE HOUSE WOULD BE SO CHEERY IF YOU WERE THERE, AYAKO...

YUMMY...

WELL THEN, I'LL MAKE SURE TO BRING YOU YOUR NEW YEAR'S K'MONO AND CLOGS ON THE EVE...

YAY, SIS!!

YOUNG MISSUS! IT'S THE MASTA!

PLEASE HURRY, IT MIGHT'VE BEEN A STROKE!

HE WAS WATCHIN' 'EM POUND MOCHI IN DA YARD WHEN HE SUDDENLY COLLAPSED!

SUMMON DOCTOR YAMA-ZAKI! HURRY!

'TWAS A STROKE, INDEED.

DOCTOR, WHAT OUGHT WE DO?

FIRST, TOTAL BED REST! I'LL RUN BLOOD TESTS, 'N WE'LL SEE...

WILL HE RE-COVER?

WHETHER HE DOES OR NOT IS UP T'FATE, BUT EV'N IF HE DOES, IT AIN'T GONNA BE PRETTY.

ICHIRO, YA GONNA HAVE T'STEP UP 'N BE STRONG!

PA... PLEASE DON'T DIE...

PLEASE DON'T DIE. AYAKO IS WAITING FOR YOU. YOU'RE THE ONLY ONE SHE CAN COUNT ON.

FATHER, REMEMBER YOUR PROMISE TO ME... AYAKO'S ONLY HOPE IS TO BE LET OUTSIDE ON NEW YEAR'S DAY...

ALL O' YA, STOP LOOKIN' SO MOURNFUL! MA'S TH' ONLY ONE NEEDED FER PA'S CARE!

TH' REST O' YA, PREPARE FER NEW YEAR'S!

HMPH, HOW DARE HE DO THIS NOW, AT SUCH A BUSY TIME!

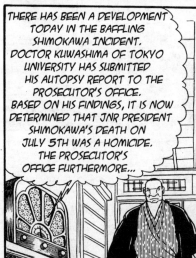

THERE HAS BEEN A DEVELOPMENT TODAY IN THE BAFFLING SHIMOKAWA INCIDENT. DOCTOR KUWASHIMA OF TOKYO UNIVERSITY HAS SUBMITTED HIS AUTOPSY REPORT TO THE PROSECUTOR'S OFFICE. BASED ON HIS FINDINGS, IT IS NOW DETERMINED THAT JNR PRESIDENT SHIMOKAWA'S DEATH ON JULY 5TH WAS A HOMICIDE. THE PROSECUTOR'S OFFICE FURTHERMORE...

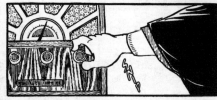

IF PA SHOULD KICK TH' BUCKET WHILE LIKE THIS, WHAT'S GONNA HAPPEN WIT' HIS BEQUEST?!

NOTE: THE REFRAIN IS FROM THE 1949 HIT SONG "GINZA KAN KAN MUSUME."

PA'S A VEGETABLE NOW, MA. WHAT THEY CALL A LIVIN' CORPSE.

HE MIGHT'VE BEEN BETTER OFF IF TH' STROKE HAD JUST KILLED HIM.

HOW DARE YA!!

TH' THING I REGRET MOST, THOUGH, IS NOT HAVIN' ASKED PA ...

HOW HE INTENDED 'DISTRIBUTE HIS ASSETS.

'COURSE, IF YA ASK ME, MA, I THINK AS FIRST SON, I OUGHTA INHERIT TH' FAMILY PROPERTY.

WHERE'S THAT PAPER ?!!

THAT AIN'T NECESSARILY GONNA BE THE CASE, ICHIRO. YA SEE, PA'S LONG DECIDED WHO'LL GET WHAT, 'N WRITTEN IT ALL DOWN.

287

CHAPTER 11

THE SHADOW OF UPHEAVAL

290

291

HONEY?

WHERE ARE YOU CALLING FROM?

ARE YOU AT THAT REDHEAD BLABER'S PLACE AGAIN?!

YES, WHAT ABOUT IT?

IT'S FOR OUR SURVIVAL, REMEMBER?

YOU CAN'T WORK AT ALL, SO I HAVE TO WORK LIKE A HORSE TO MAKE ENOUGH FOR BOTH OF US.

I KNOW!! BUT IT'S DANGEROUS TO KEEP GOING IN AND OUT OF A U.S. BASE!

HAVE YOU FORGOTTEN THAT THE ORGAN IS OUT THERE LOOKING FOR US?!

BUT MY ONLY MARKETABLE SKILL IS MY ENGLISH.

I NEVER TOLD YOU TO BECOME AN OFFICER'S LOVER!!

MM... JEALOUS?

S.H.H

WHY WOULD I BE JEALOUS?! I DON'T CARE A WHIT ABOUT YOU!

I'M JUST AFRAID THEY'D UNCOVER MY TRUE IDENTITY.

I'LL STAY AT THE CAPTAIN'S TONIGHT... YOU CAN HAVE SOME PEACE AND QUIET!

SLAM

WENCH!

IT'S BEEN ALMOST A YEAR SINCE I FLED HOME...

THE POLICE WANT ME, THE CIC'S AFTER ME... IT'S A WONDER I'M STILL AROUND.

TRUTH IS, I'D REALLY LIKE TO CUT MY TIES WITH HER!

I JUST CAN'T TRUST THAT WOMAN...

THIS IS LAME...

I CAN'T KEEP LIVING LIKE THIS...

MA... NAOKO... WHAT'S HAPPENED SINCE I LEFT?

AND SHIRO... DO YOU STILL CONDEMN ME?

AND... AYAKO!

I DO FEEL SORRY FOR YOU.

NOTE: THE VISITOR'S STILTED SPEECH AND HIS NAME ("KIN" USES THE CHARACTER FOR "KIM") SUGGEST A KOREAN BACKGROUND.

YOU WANT FLEE JAPAN, YES? I KNOW YOU SITUATION, YOU SURROUNDED BY ENEMIES.

YOU MAKE MISTAKE, TO TEAM UP WITH CIC.

WHO THE HELL ARE YOU ?!

I FRIEND. I THINK, I HELP YOU ESCAPE.

...

I GIVE YOU MONEY, PASSPORT TOO.

I DON'T KNOW WHOSE AGENT YOU ARE...

BUT NO THANKS. I'D RATHER NOT BE LURED OUT AND STRANGLED.

I SEE, I BE FRANK TO YOU. I WANT YOU KILL AMERICAN.

HUH ?

YOU WIFE CAN DO IT.

YOU KNOW WHAT MY WIFE'S BEEN UP TO?

297

JUNE 25

SHE RE-TURNS.

I'VE BEEN THINKING THINGS OVER. I'M TIRED OF LIVING LIKE THIS. LET'S GO TO BRAZIL OR SOMEWHERE AND START FRESH FROM SCRATCH.

OH? AND WHERE ARE WE GETTING THE MONEY FOR BRAZIL?

GET SOME CONSOLATION MONEY FROM BLABER!

SO NOW YOU THINK YOU'RE MY PIMP?

SINCE YOU ALREADY SLEEP WITH HIM NOT FOR LOVE BUT FOR SURVIVAL, HOW HARD COULD IT BE?

I'M GOING TO DO NO SUCH THING!

HE'S A GOOD MAN.

SLAP

ENOUGH WITH THIS FARCE!

IT'S TIME TO COME CLEAN.

DO WE KEEP PRETENDING TO BE MARRIED AND CONTINUE THIS LIFE OF SNEAKING AROUND, EACH OF US WITH A GUILTY CONSCIENCE... OR SHALL WE TRULY SETTLE THINGS UP AND START OUR LIVES OVER FOR REAL?

THANKS TO BOTH OF US HAVING DONE DIRTY WORK FOR THE AMERICANS, WE'RE NOT ABLE TO TRUST EACH OTHER. TIME TO BURY ALL THAT, TOO.

YOU'RE RIGHT.

THIS IS OUR CHANCE TO SETTLE UP.

THE CAPTAIN TOLD ME HE WAS BEING REASSIGNED... SO I'LL END THINGS WITH HIM, LIKE YOU SAID.

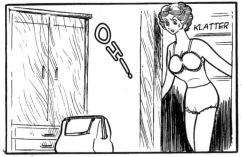

302

RANT

WEE!OOO

A POSTAL MONEY ORDER FOR 500,000 YEN?!

YES. THE PAYEE IS AYAKO TENGE.

IF AYAKO'S NOT ABLE TO PICK IT UP HERSELF...

PLEASE DESIGNATE A PROXY PAYEE.

CAN YOU PUT DOWN IBA TENGE? I-B-A... SHE IS AYAKO'S MOTHER.

KRITK

JUST THIS MORNING, THE NORTH KOREAN ARMY INVADED THE REPUBLIC OF KOREA, CROSSING THE 38TH PARALLEL IN 11 PLACES! FIERCE FIGHTING APPEARS TO BE ONGOING...

SORRY TO TROUBLE YOU, SIS...

SHH... YOU KNOW HOW SHARP MY HUSBAND'S HEARING IS...

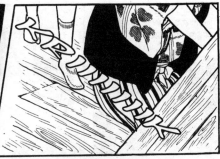

SHE'S NOT TOO HAGGARD...

NO. I WORRIED ABOUT THE DAMPNESS, BUT IT'S QUITE DRY DOWN HERE. AND THE SKYLIGHT LETS IN AT LEAST 4 HOURS OF SUN EVERY DAY.

YOU POOR, POOR THING...

TO HAVE TO SPEND YOUR ENTIRE LIFE DOWN HERE...

IF FATHER WERE WELL, THERE WOULD BE A WAY TO SAVE HER...

BUT MY HUSBAND LOATHES AND DESPISES HER, SO THERE'S NO CHANCE OF IT AT THIS POINT.

307

I'M SHOCKED AT HOW CALM YOU SEEM, SIS! SHE'S YOUR OWN CHILD!

DO YOU REALLY THINK I'M FINE?

I'VE CRIED MYSELF DRY...

THIS IS THE ONLY WAY... I CAN MAINTAIN MY POSITION AS WIFE.

AYAKO... IT'S ME, NAOKO SIS. WE WON'T BE SEEING EACH OTHER FOR A LONG TIME.

YOU SEE, A WAR'S STARTED IN KOREA, SO THOSE MEAN AMERICANS AND THEIR LACKEY OFFICIALS ARE CHASING AFTER SIS AND HER FRIENDS TO THROW US IN JAIL.

SO I'M GONNA GO PLAY HIDE-AND-SEEK... SIS WILL FIGHT TO THE END...

YOU NEED TO HANG IN THERE, TOO. DON'T YOU GIVE IN TO THIS FAMILY'S HORRIBLE CUSTOMS OR POWER!

'BYE...

KRII-KRIIIII-KRII

YOU BE WELL, OKAY, SIS...?

GIVE MY REGARDS TO SHIRO.

LEAVING ALREADY?

BE SAFE.

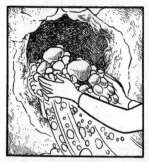

SHOVE

SHOVE
SHOVE

SHIRO
BIG
BRO
!!

...
AYAKO
!

...

HOW'VE
YOU
BEEN
...?

315

THIS IS THE EIGHTH TIME. THE FIRST WAS FOR 500,000 YEN! SINCE THEN, A FEW TIMES A YEAR... SOMETIMES 300,000 YEN, OTHER TIMES 200,000...

MA'S BEEN QUIETLY DEPOSITING IT IN A BANK... BUT IT'S ALL YOURS, AYAKO.

WHO'S IT FROM?

THE SENDER'S NAME IS GIBBERISH, BUT I'VE GOT A HUNCH. I'M PRETTY SURE IT'S... JIRO BIG BRO.

LATER.

MAMA...

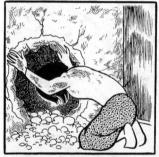

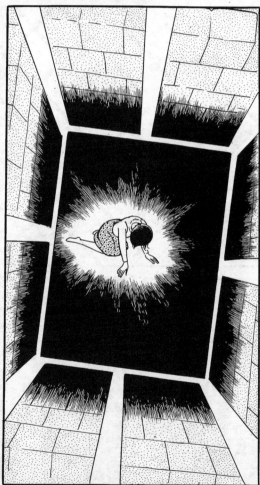

IT'S BEEN 7 YEARS ALREADY, SINCE HE COLLAPSED?

TIME FLIES.

7 YEARS LIKE THIS, WIT'OUT CHANGE. WHY WON'T HE JUST GIVE UP ?!!

I FEEL BAD FER YA.

I WISH HE'D JUST UP 'N CROAK ALREADY!

FOOL! IF YER PA PASSES INTO TH' AFTERLIFE NOW, THERE'LL BE A FEEDIN' FRENZY O'ER TH' INHERITANCE.

SEEMS PA'D PREPARED A WILL AHEAD O' TIME N' ENTRUSTED IT T'MA...

IT OUTLINES ASSET DISTRIBUTION.

WHAT? THAT'S NEWS T'ME! SO, WHEN'S TH' OLD WOMAN GONNA SHOW IT T'YA?

DOC, YA GOTS YER EYE ON A PIECE O' TH' PIE, TOO?

'COURSE, I MAY BE A DISTANT RELATION, BUT I STILL SHARE BLOOD WIT' YER PA!

THEN I'LL LETS YA IN ON IT, DOC. YA SEE, MA'S SUPPOSED T'BRING OUT TH' TESTAMENT 'N SHOW IT T'US WHEN AYAKO TURNS 15!

AYAKO ?!

AYAKO ...STILL BE ALIVE?

I THOUGHT SHE BE LONG DEAD...

SHH !!

SHE AIN'T DEAD YET.

UNBELIEVABLE... SHE BEEN IN A CELLAR 7 YEARS, WIT'OUT SEEIN' TH' LIGHT O' DAY, 'N STILL LIVES...

I'M REAL INTRIGUED, PROFESSIONALLY SPEAKIN'.

FOOL! FOOL! DON'T YA SPILL A WORD T'ANYONE! IF TH' POLICE OR TOWN OFFICE FIND OUT, WE'RE DONE FER.

HOW LONG SHE STAYIN' IN THERE?

UNTIL SHE DIES, O' COURSE...

POOR THING... THERE AIN'T ANY RECOURSE T'LET HER OUT?

REMEMBER TH' CLAN MEET? AYAKO NEEDS TO DIE FER TH' SAKE O' TH' FAMILY!

WELL, YEAH, BUT...

YA SQUEAK AT ALL, 'N I'LL CUT YA OFF!

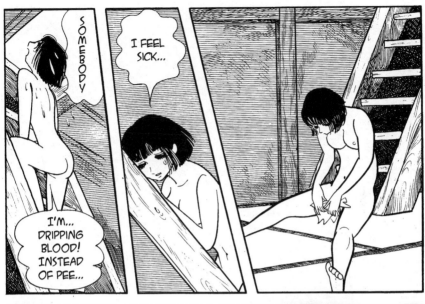

CHAPTER 12

CHRYSALIS

APRIL 1956, TOKYO

WE'RE HERE.

BOSS, HAVE ONE OF THEM KIDS DO SUCH SIMPLE TASKS AS MAILIN' MONEY OUT.

KINJO, YOU SHOULD KNOW BY NOW THAT THIS, I LIKE TAKING CARE OF PERSONALLY.

STUBBORN AS EVER.

POSTAL MONEY ORDER FOR 500,000 YEN.

TO AYAKO, C/O MRS. IBA TENGE OF FURUHATA IN NAKAKAMIGATA, YODOYAMA CITY, AOMORI?

VERY WELL, SIR.

MR. JIRO TENGE?

SORRY, WRONG PERSON. I AM TOMIO YUTENJI OF THE OUSHINKAI...

BUT YOUR REAL NAME IS TENGE, NO? YOU'RE FROM YODOYAMA?

I AM GETA, INVESTIGATIONS SECTION 1 CHIEF OF THE METRO POLICE.

AH YES, I KNOW YOU. MY YOUNGER ASSOCIATES ARE OFTEN IN YOUR CARE...

SO, HOW CAN I HELP YOU? WHAT ABOUT THIS TENGE FELLOW?

WELL... IT'S NO GREAT EMERGENCY, BUT DO YOU RECALL A TANUMA FROM YODOYAMA POLICE STATION, WHO WAS PURSUING YOU 7 YEARS AGO?

NO CLUE.

I SEE. HE HAD MARKED YOU 7 YEARS AGO AS A SUSPECT IN THE YODOYAMA INCIDENT, BUT YOU SKIPPED TOWN JUST AS HE WAS CLOSING IN ON YOU...

THAT'S GOT NAUGHT TO DO WITH ME, SO STOP THESE FALSE ACCUSATIONS.

MR. TANUMA'S NOW GOT ESOPHAGEAL CANCER, AND ONLY HAS ONE MONTH TO LIVE.

AND SO HE'S ASKED ME TO TAKE OVER THIS CALLING OF HIS.

OF COURSE, I HAVEN'T RECEIVED ANY FORMAL ORDERS FROM MY SUPERIORS...

NOR CAN I FILE ANY PAPERS.

BUT I'M GOING TO BE LOOKING INTO YOU GOOD...

MR. INSPECTOR, DESIST OR I SHALL SUE YOU FOR CIVIL RIGHTS VIOLATIONS.

NO WORRIES, MR. TENGE.

ONCE I HAVE MY PROOF, YOU'LL BE SUMMONED.

MY NAME IS NOT TENGE! I AM TOMIO YUTENJI!

WHAT BE THE MATTER, BOSS?

NOTHING. THIS STUPID IDIOT WANTED TO TALK TO ME.

329

SOME METRO POLICE SECTION CHIEF... HE KNEW MY REAL NAME.

TENGE?

DON'T YOU WORRY ABOUT IT NONE.

SO LONG AS YOU KEEP ACTING DUMB, IT'LL BLOW OVER.

YEAH...

I AM THE ONLY ONE WHO KNOWS THE REAL YOU, O' 7 YEARS AGO.

THAT'S RIGHT. JUST YOU, KINJO...

I WAS REBORN, WHEN I TEAMED UP WITH YOU AND MADE A LOAD OFF OF THE KOREAN WAR.

WHERE TO, BOSS?

CLUB MEMORY.

Nightclub Memory

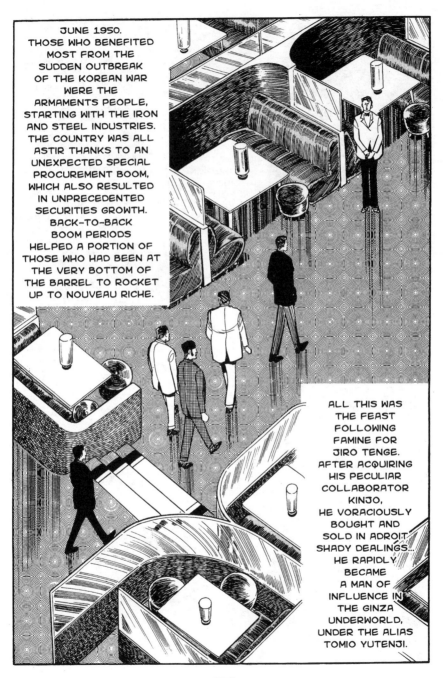

JUNE 1950. THOSE WHO BENEFITED MOST FROM THE SUDDEN OUTBREAK OF THE KOREAN WAR WERE THE ARMAMENTS PEOPLE, STARTING WITH THE IRON AND STEEL INDUSTRIES. THE COUNTRY WAS ALL ASTIR THANKS TO AN UNEXPECTED SPECIAL PROCUREMENT BOOM, WHICH ALSO RESULTED IN UNPRECEDENTED SECURITIES GROWTH. BACK-TO-BACK BOOM PERIODS HELPED A PORTION OF THOSE WHO HAD BEEN AT THE VERY BOTTOM OF THE BARREL TO ROCKET UP TO NOUVEAU RICHE.

ALL THIS WAS THE FEAST FOLLOWING FAMINE FOR JIRO TENGE. AFTER ACQUIRING HIS PECULIAR COLLABORATOR KINJO, HE VORACIOUSLY BOUGHT AND SOLD IN ADROIT SHADY DEALINGS... HE RAPIDLY BECAME A MAN OF INFLUENCE IN THE GINZA UNDERWORLD, UNDER THE ALIAS TOMIO YUTENJI.

WITH THE KOREAN WAR IN A STALEMATE AND THE TREATY OF SAN FRANCISCO SIGNED, THE WORLD BEGAN CHANGING AT A DIZZYING RATE. LEFT-WING FORCES WENT UNDERGROUND FOLLOWING THE RED PURGE. YOUTH REPEATEDLY CAUSED SOCIAL PROBLEMS THANKS TO THEIR WARPED POST-WAR EDUCATION, AND DECADENT CRIMES CONTINUED TO OCCUR AROUND THE U.S. BASES.

AMIDST ALL THIS, MEMORIES OF SOME TRAGEDIES FADED ...

OF THE SHIMOKAWA, MITAKA, AND MATSUKAWA INCIDENTS ...

AND OF THE YODOYAMA INCIDENT ...

AND ITS SADDEST VICTIM, AYAKO...

CHK
CHK
CHK
CHK
CHK
CHK

1961, YODOYAMA

333

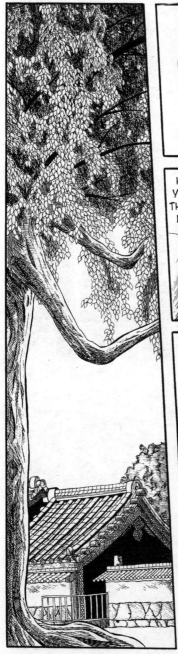

HOW DO YOU READ THIS WORD, BIG SIS?

PREG-NANCY.

AYAKO!! WHO IN THE WORLD BROUGHT YOU THIS WOMEN'S MAGAZINE?!!

SHIRO BIG BRO.

SHAME ON HIM!!

335

336

WHOSE ... CHILD AM I?

JOLT!

YOU MUSTN'T KNOW! DON'T ASK ANY QUESTIONS ABOUT THE WORLD OR OUR FAMILY, FOR YOUR OWN SAKE!

NAW, I WANNA KNOW!! I WANNA LEAVE! RIGHT NOW!

FOOL! DON'T YOU UNDERSTAND THAT IF YOU LEAVE HERE, YOU'LL BE KILLED?!

I WANNA LEAVE! PLEASE LET ME OUT!

MOVE!

AYAKO, WAIT!

339

AYAKO...

YOU ASLEEP?

WHAT HAPPENED THIS AFTERNOON? SIS-IN-LAW CAME BACK T' THE HOUSE ALL RED-EYED 'N PUFFY-FACED.

YA OUGHTN'T GIVE HER A HARD TIME,

AYA...

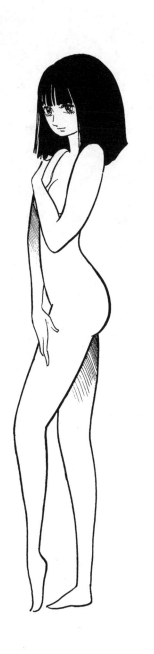

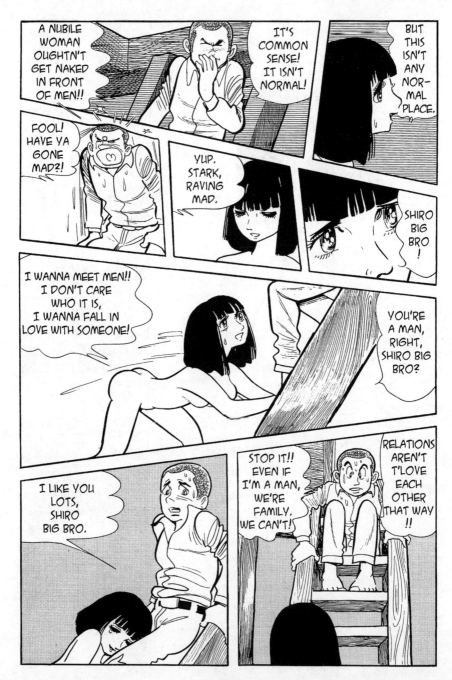

343

J—JUST THIS ONCE, YA HEAR, AYAKO? I'LL DO THIS FOR YA JUST ONE TIME...

SHI-
RO.

SHIRO!
CAN'T
YA
HEAR
ME?

I NEEDS T'TALK T'YA AFTER LUNCH.

WHAT UP? WHY NOT RIGHT NOW?

NOT IN FRONT O' MA. COME TAKE A WALK WIT' ME.

...

WATER'S BOILED!

YA ALL COME 'N EAT ...

MA, I'M BORROWIN' SHIRO FER A BIT.

BZZP

CHK CHK CHK

BNNP

CHK CHK

HOW FAR WE GOING ...?

NOTE: "NIGHT CRAWLING" WAS (AND MAY STILL BE) A CUSTOM IN RURAL JAPAN WHERE A YOUNG MAN, USUALLY WITH THE CONSENT OF HIS TARGET'S PARENTS, SNEAKS INTO A YOUNG WOMAN'S BEDROOM TO ENGAGE IN SEX WITH HER.

EVEN KNOCKIN' UP TENANT FARMERS' WOMEN...

EACH TIME HUSHIN' THEM UP WITH OUR MONEY 'N POWER.

DID'JA KNOW O-RYO CAME FROM OUR PA SLEEPIN' WITH GOSUKE'S WIFE BACK WHEN HE WAS YOUNGER?

NONE O' THAT BE ANY O' YER BUSINESS!

DON'T TOUCH AYAKO AGAIN!

YER SAYIN' I OUGHTA BE THE ONLY SAINT IN OUR FAMILY?

THAT AIN'T GONNA BE.

I JUST WANT AYAKO, WHO BEEN IN THAT GRAVE FOR 11 YEARS LIKE SOME BEETLE CHRYSALIS...

T'BE ABLE T'ENJOY A LI'L TASTE OF LIFE!

CHAPTER 13

THE DOLLHOUSE

354

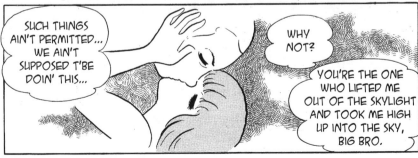

SUCH THINGS AIN'T PERMITTED... WE AIN'T SUPPOSED T'BE DOIN' THIS...

WHY NOT?

YOU'RE THE ONE WHO LIFTED ME OUT OF THE SKYLIGHT AND TOOK ME HIGH UP INTO THE SKY, BIG BRO.

356

357

BUT THIS... IS THE ONLY TIME I CAN ESCAPE FROM HERE, INTO THE STARRY NIGHT...

YOU TRY TO ALWAYS DRAG ME RIGHT BACK IN...

TOMORROW'S YER BIRTHDAY, AYAKO. YER GONNA TURN 15.

SO I'VE BEEN TOLD. I DON'T REALLY CARE.

MA'S GONNA BRING OUT 'N READ PA'S DEED TOMORROW.

YEAH?

SHE'S T'SHOW US WHEN YA TURN 15 TH' PAPER THAT SAYS HOW PA'S FORTUNE'S GETTIN' PARCELED OUT.

PA'S STILL BEDRIDDEN?

YUP... WIT'OUT AWARENESS.

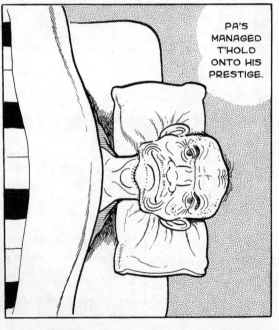

PA'S MANAGED T'HOLD ONTO HIS PRESTIGE.

BUT... EVEN WIT'OUT ANY AWARENESS...

358

FER REAL? DAT'S UN-BELIEVABLE.

EY? WHAT'S DAT?

HEYA ALL, THANKS FER COMIN'... SINCE PA STILL BE IN TH' STATE HE'S IN, I'LL BE READIN' TH' DEED IN HIS PLACE...

MISTA ICHIRO, IT TRUE AYAKO STILL BE ALIVE?

NAW, THEY BE SAYIN' AYAKO STILL BE ALIVE, INSIDE DAT CELLAR...

NO WAY!

DAT BE NONSENSE... IT BEEN 11 WHOLE YEARS SINCE DAT DAY!

FOOL! AYAKO BE LONG DEAD.

IT JUST BE THAT IF SHE WERE STILL LIVIN', SHE BE TURNIN' 15 TODAY.

MA! BRING OUT TH' DEED!

SURE.

IT BE ...

...INSIDE PA'S PILLOW...

360

DARN, THAT BE WHERE IT WAS? NO WONDER I COULDN'T FIND IT!

BUT NO MATTER, I KNOW IT'LL SAY...

THAT I'LL BE GETTIN' TH' MAJORITY O' HIS ASSETS.

'N SO ...

...IT BE...

MISTA ICHIRO, WHAT BE DA MATTER? JUST READ IT, WILL YA.

WHAT IT SAY?

N-NO, THAT AIN'T POSSIBLE!!

SU'E !!

YES?

WHAT THIS BE?

THIS FARCE !!

FWAP!!

HE BE GIVIN' 80% O' HIS ASSETS T'AYAKO'S BIRTH MOTHER ?!

DAMMIT!

WELL, DAT BE DA MISSUS.

'N DAT MAKES PERFECT SENSE.

SHADDUP!

WHAT
...

AM I
...

SUPPOSED
T'DO?!

SU'E...
HEH HEH
HEH HEH
...

AYAKO'S
BIRTH MOTHER...
YA GOT
PA'S ASSETS.
YA HAPPY
NOW?

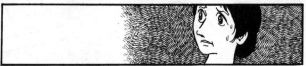

NOW
WRITE!

WRITE
WHAT
?

A WIFE'S
PROPERTY
BELONGS
T'HER
HUSBAND!

IT BE
NATURAL FER
A HUSBAND
T'RECEIVE
HIS WIFE'S
FORTUNE.
YUP.

'CUZ
YER MY
WOMAN
...

YER
GONNA
SIGN IT
ALL O'ER
T'ME.

NO.

WHAT?!

WHA
CHA
JUST
SAY
?!

365

I AM TAKING FATHER'S MONEY. IT BELONGS TO AYAKO AND ME.

I'LL ALSO TAKE AYAKO WITH ME. SHE'S NOT YOUR CHILD, SO THAT'S OKAY, EY.

GO AHEAD! YA'LL BE RIDDIN' US O' A PLAGUE!

DO YOU SEE MO- THER?

SHE'S SEEIN' OFF TH' RELATIONS. NO NEED T'SAY GOOD- BYE T'HER!

HEY... SU'E... WON'T YA JUST THINK IT O'ER, EY? I NEED YA. FOR MY FIELDS...

YOU DON'T NEED ME. YOU NEED THE MONEY.

SU'E ...

368

WOMEN BE SO FASCINATIN'. GIVE 'EM A BIT O' MONEY, 'N THEIR PERSON SUDDENLY CHANGES.

YA NEV'R WOULD'VE DARED SHOW SUCH ATTITUDE, AFORE.

AYE, I'VE FINALLY FOUND TH' STRENGTH,

T'MOVE ON WITH AYAKO, NO LONGER 'PENDIN' ON...

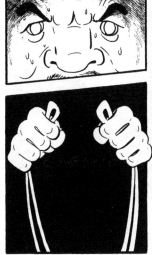

UGH ...

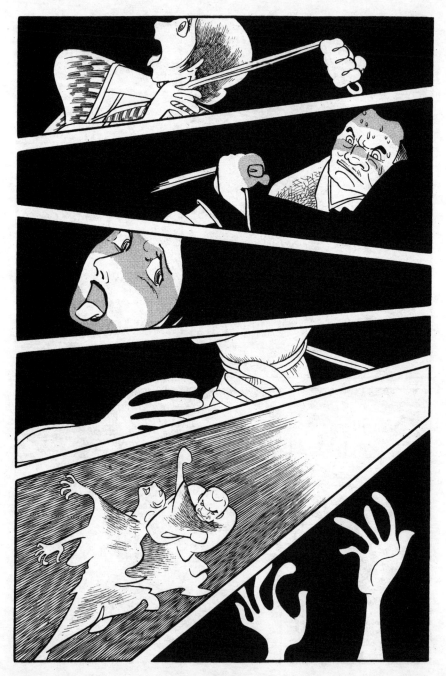

KLATTER

Y-YA GOT SOME-THIN' T'SAY, PA?!

HMPH!

AH... ICHIRO... WHERE'S SU'E...?

SU'E? SHE UP 'N LEFT WHILE YA WERE OUT, MA.

S-SAID SHE AIN'T EV'R COMIN' BACK.

DID THAT GIRL

REALLY, TRULY LEAVE?

YUP, SAYIN' ON HER WAY OUT SHE'LL HAND PA'S ASSETS O'ER T'ME.

SU'E...
REST IN
PEACE,
EY...

YA'LL POISON YER-SELF.

MIGHT BE TH' AGIN', BUT I AIN'T SLEEPIN' MUCH, MAKIN' ME CHAFE.

IT BEEN A MONTH ALREADY. WHY DON'T YA GO SEE DOC YAMAZAKI?

NAW!

THAT YAMAZAKI'S A WILY OLD FOX. HE BE PLOTTIN' SOMETHIN' REGARDIN' TH' ASSET DISTRIBUTION.

HE'S A HIGHBROW, THERE BE NO KNOWIN' WHAT HE'D DO IN A PINCH!

YA REALLY OUGHTN'T BE SO DISTRUSTFUL O' OTHERS, ICHIRO.

YEAH? BUT JUST TH' OTHER DAY...

HE WAS LISTENIN' REAL HARD AT TH' STORE-HOUSE!

HE'S TH' ONLY ONE WHO KNOWS FER SURE AYAKO'S ALIVE.

CHAPTER 14

MUDFLOW

NOVEMBER 1961

FRUITIN' GOOD THIS YEAR, TOO...

BY TH' WAY, EY, ICHIRO...

WON'T YA LET ME SEE AYAKO, JUST ONCE?

WHAT ?!

NO WAY, DOC!

'N STOP MENTIONIN' AYAKO!

AYAKO'S GONE!

BUT IN ACTUALITY, SHE'S STILL ALIVE, EY?

IT'S MIRACULOUS, TRULY.

ISOLATED FROM TH' WORLD 12 YEARS, WIT' ONLY A LI'L LIGHT FROM A SKYLIGHT 'N SOME FOOD!

'N TH' ONLY PEOPLE T'HAVE SEEN HER BEIN' MISS SU'E 'N NAOKO, WHO'RE GONE, 'N SHIRO...

SO, YER MA'S TAKIN' CARE O' HER NOW?

SHIRO TOO.

WHY HAVEN'T YA GONE?

GUILTY CONSCIENCE?

QUIT TALKIN' 'BOUT AYAKO ALREADY!!

WON'T YA LET ME GIVE AYAKO A PHYSICAL, JUST ONCE?

I'D LIKE T'SEE HOW SHE'S DEVELOPED.

P-PROFES-
SIONALLY
SPEAKIN',
O'
COURSE.

IF YA DARE
STEP INSIDE
THAT
STOREHOUSE,
THERE'LL BE HELL
T'PAY, DOC!!

ALL RIGHT,
ALL
RIGHT...
TAKE IT
EASY.

YER REAL
PRICKLY
THESE
DAYS,
EY...

WHOO   WHOOO

HIS HEART'S GOTTEN QUITE WEAK. HARD T'SAY IF HE CAN WINTER, MISSUS IBA.

HE BEEN LIKE THIS SO LONG... I SHAN'T HAVE ANY REGRETS.

I BET NURSIN' HIM'S BEEN HARD WORK. YA GOT MY SYMPATHIES.

THANK YA MUCH, DOC.

ICHIRO AIN'T HOME TODAY?

NAW, WENT INTO TOWN.

381

EEK!

THERE, THERE, RELAX.

I'M...YER PA'S DOCTOR, YAMAZAKI. 'N I BELIEVE I'M A PATERNAL UNCLE O' YOURS.

MY-MY... HOW YA'VE GROWN ...

LAST TIME I SAW YA, YA WERE JUST A CHILD, A WEE LI'L TODDLER...

...

BY TH' WAY, YA KNOW HOW T'WRITE?

I NEED YA T'PUT YER NAME 'N THUMBPRINT ON THIS PIECE O' PAPER.

THIS HERE'S A DEED, YA SEE...

IT STATES THAT I'LL PROTECT YER FORTUNE FROM YER RELATIONS...

WHO ARE GONNA SWOOP DOWN 'N TRY T'SUCK YA DRY.

NOW SIGN RIGHT HERE.

THAT MEANS, WRITE YER NAME!

HURRY UP! CAN'T YA SEE I'M ON YER SIDE?!

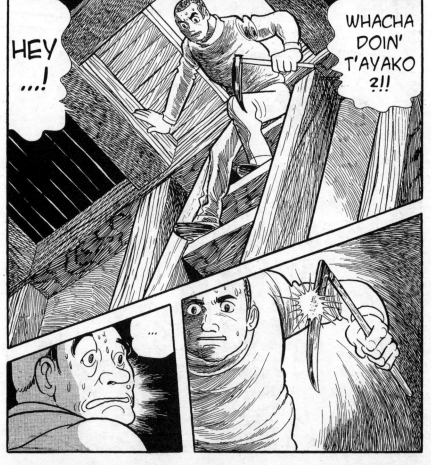

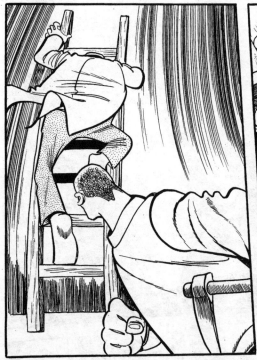

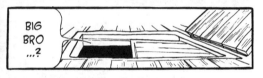

389

JUST ANSWER THIS FER ME, AYAKO. DID HE DO T'YA WHAT I ALWAYS DO WIT' YA?

NO...

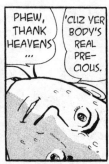

PHEW, THANK HEAVENS...

'CUZ YER BODY'S REAL PRECIOUS.

YOU'RE THE ONLY ONE I WANT, BIG BRO!

I WON'T LET ANYONE ELSE TOUCH ME!

AYAKO... LET'S GET YA OUT OF HERE!

PA'S A LIVIN' CORPSE, 'N ICHIRO BIG BRO'S A DRUNKARD WHO STARTS IMBIBIN' AT FIRST LIGHT 'TIL HIS MIND GOES.

PLUS, I GOT THIS HUNCH SIS-IN-LAW DIDN'T JUST UP 'N LEAVE...

THIS TENGE FAMILY'S COMIN' T'AN END.

I CAN JUST FEEL IT CREAKIN' 'N STARTIN' T'GIVE OUT.

'N THAT'S FINE WIT' ME. IN FACT, I WISH IT'D HAPPENED SOONER. IT'S BEST THAT SUCH A MOLD-INFESTED DIRTY FAMILY LINE BE DESTROYED.

DIE, ALL OF YA WHO DID THIS T'AYAKO!! DIE IN SOME DITCH 'N GO T'HELL!!

...

I WANNA STAY HERE.

IS IT REALLY... THAT TERRI-FYIN'?

POOR THING... IT'S OKAY. JUST STAY RIGHT THERE.

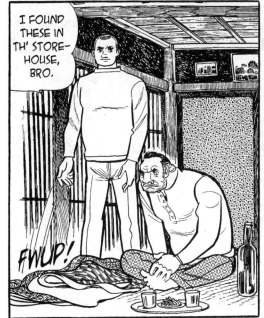

I FOUND THESE IN TH' STOREHOUSE, BRO.

FWUP!

...

SOMETHIN' TERRIBLE HAPPENED T'SIS-IN-LAW INSIDE TH' STOREHOUSE, AM I RIGHT?

I'VE GOT A PRETTY GOOD IDEA WHAT.

...

SHIRO! YA IMP.

WHACHA WANTIN' T'SAY?

396

I BELIEVE THERE'S A TYPE OF WAR CRIMES CHARGE CALLED "CRIMES AGAINST HUMANITY."

SO WHAT IS HUMANITY? 'N DO THOSE DOIN' TH' JUDGIN' HAVE IT?

NOW I'M FINALLY SEEIN' THAT TH' TRIBUNAL WAS AN OPPORTUNISTIC COURT OF TH' WINNIN' SIDE.

WHAT STANDARDS IS JUSTICE BASED ON?

WHAT IS A CRIME? 'N WHO IS REALLY QUALIFIED T'BE JUDGE 'N JURY?

NO MATTER WHAT YA MIGHT'VE DONE T'SIS-IN-LAW...

DO I HAVE ANY RIGHT T'SAY SOMETHIN' 'BOUT IT?

I'M GONNA KEEP VIOLATIN' AYAKO. I MIGHT EVEN MARRY HER!

 YA SEE... I VOLUNTARILY BECAME TH' TENGE GARBAGE DUMP.

 THE DUMP CAN ONLY HAVE GARBAGE PITCHED AT IT...

 IT AIN'T QUALIFIED T'JUDGE ANYONE... GOT THAT, BRO?

 COME, ICHIRO, SHIRO. YER PA JUST PASSED.

 TROMP TROMP

398

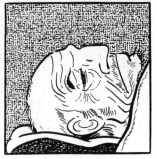

LOOK, SUCH A PEACEFUL EXPRESSION ON HIS FACE...

HAN'NYA-
HARAMITTA JI
SHÔKEN GO'UN
KAIKÛ,
DO'ISSAI'KUYAKU.
SHARISHI,
SHIKI'FUIKÛ,

KÛFU'ISHIKI.
SHIKISOKU-
ZEKÛ,
KÛSOKU-
ZESHIKI
JÛSÔ-
GYÔSEKI
YAKUBU-
NYOZE.

SHARISHI,
ZESHOHÔKÛSO.
FUSHÔFUMETSU,
FUKUFUJÔ,
FUZÔFUGEN.
ZEKOKÛCHÛ
MUSHIKI;
MUJUSÔ-
GYÔSHIKI;

403

E HAN'NYA-HARAMIT TAKO SHIN-MUKEIGA, MUKEGEKO

MU'U'KUFU. ONRI ISSAI TENDŌMUSŌ KUKYŌ NEHAN. SANZE SHOBUTSU...

MA!!

OH MY, NAOKO!

MA... SORRY FOR NOT WRITING.

NAOKO, WELCOME. THANKS FER COMIN' BACK.

GO ON, OFFER HIM SOME 'NCENSE.

ICHIRO BIG BRO...

SHIRO...

...

404

...

WHERE'S AYAKO?

IN TH' CELLAR.

STILL ?!

SHH

WHATEVER FOR? WHY CAN'T YOU LET HER OUT ?!

HOW TERRIBLE!! IT'S PA'S FUNERAL!

BOTH MA AND BROTHER ARE INSANE, I SWEAR.

405

THE TRAP-DOOR'S NAILED SHUT!!

WHAT IN THE WORLD IS GOING ON?!

WHO DID THIS?

AYAKO!! AYAKO!!

AYAKO!!

PLEASE ANSWER... AREN'T YOU IN THERE?

THIS IS ABSO-LUTELY HORRIBLE.

AYAKO!!

REMEMBER ME? IT'S ME, NAOKO, YOUR BIG SIS!!

I'M SO, SO GLAD... YOU'RE ALL RIGHT...

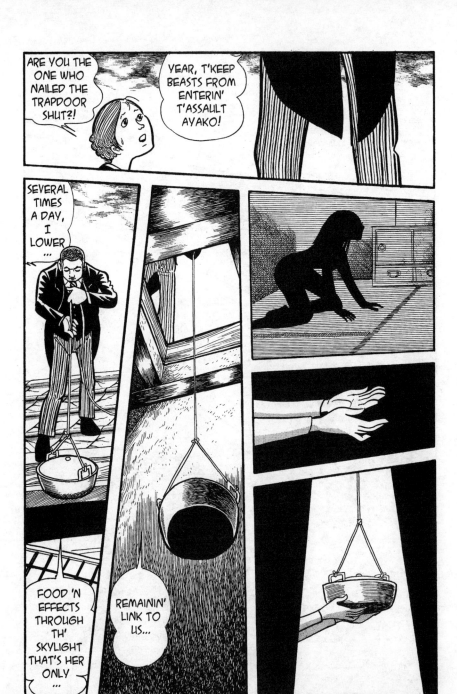

SLAP!!

...

I DON'T BLAME YA FER SLAPPIN' ME, SIS, SINCE YA WERE ALWAYS TH' MOST DECENT OF US SIBLINGS.

I THOUGHT I COULD AT LEAST TRUST YOU TO DO RIGHT BY OUR FAMILY, YOU IDIOT!!

HEARSE BE LEAVIN', SHIRO! WHERE YA BE?!

GYATEI GYATEI HARA-GYATEI HARASÔ-GYATEI

VODOYAMA
VALLEYTOP
CREMATORIUM

I'VE BEEN WORKING AS A NANNY AT A FRIEND'S OUT TOWARDS SENKAI VILLAGE.

'N WHEN DID YA ACQUIRE YER HUSBAND?

5 YEARS AGO.

5 YEARS ALREADY?

I HAD NO IDEA ...

YA OUGHTA HAVE BROUGHT HIM.

BUT I'M PRACTICALLY A STRANGER HERE.

NAOKO, WON'T YA COME BACK?

SINCE SU'E LEFT, I BEEN SO, SO TERRIBLY LONELY...

'N NOW THAT PA'S GONE...

CHAPTER 15

LIGHT AND SHADOW

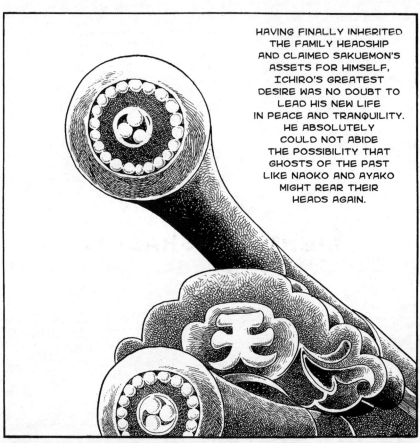

HAVING FINALLY INHERITED THE FAMILY HEADSHIP AND CLAIMED SAKUEMON'S ASSETS FOR HIMSELF, ICHIRO'S GREATEST DESIRE WAS NO DOUBT TO LEAD HIS NEW LIFE IN PEACE AND TRANQUILITY. HE ABSOLUTELY COULD NOT ABIDE THE POSSIBILITY THAT GHOSTS OF THE PAST LIKE NAOKO AND AYAKO MIGHT REAR THEIR HEADS AGAIN.

ICHIRO EVENTUALLY TOOK A NEW BRIDE, ONE SO BLAND AND DEVOID OF A ROLE IN THIS TALE THAT SHE IS NOT WORTH INTRODUCING HERE.

TURNING AWAY EVEN THIS NEW WIFE, SHIRO MONOPOLIZED THE CELLAR-DWELLING AYAKO.

BUILT INTO HIS ROUTINE WAS THE TASK OF DELIVERING FOOD AND SUNDRY TO AYAKO THREE TIMES A DAY VIA THE STOREHOUSE'S SKYLIGHT.

AND SO NOW ONLY HE WAS WITNESS TO HER GROWTH.

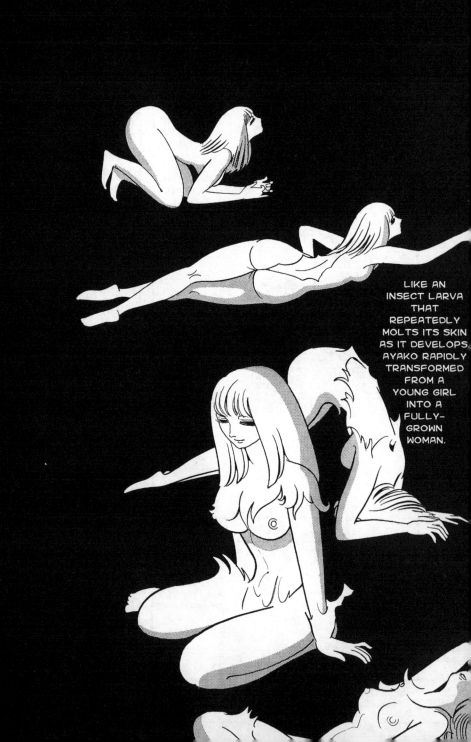

LIKE AN INSECT LARVA THAT REPEATEDLY MOLTS ITS SKIN AS IT DEVELOPS, AYAKO RAPIDLY TRANSFORMED FROM A YOUNG GIRL INTO A FULLY-GROWN WOMAN.

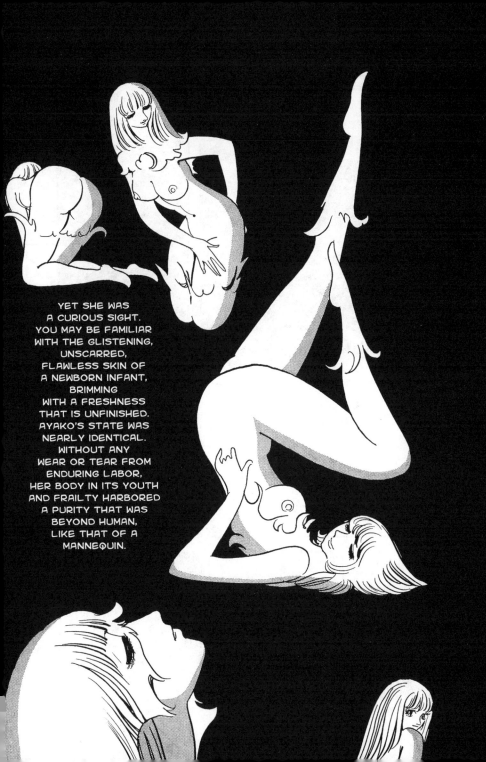

YET SHE WAS
A CURIOUS SIGHT.
YOU MAY BE FAMILIAR
WITH THE GLISTENING,
UNSCARRED,
FLAWLESS SKIN OF
A NEWBORN INFANT,
BRIMMING
WITH A FRESHNESS
THAT IS UNFINISHED.
AYAKO'S STATE WAS
NEARLY IDENTICAL.
WITHOUT ANY
WEAR OR TEAR FROM
ENDURING LABOR,
HER BODY IN ITS YOUTH
AND FRAILTY HARBORED
A PURITY THAT WAS
BEYOND HUMAN,
LIKE THAT OF A
MANNEQUIN.

JUNE 17, 1971

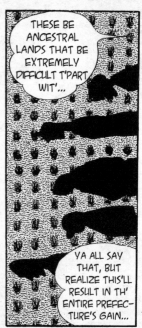

THESE BE ANCESTRAL LANDS THAT BE EXTREMELY DIFFICULT T'PART WIT'...

YA ALL SAY THAT, BUT REALIZE THIS'LL RESULT IN TH' ENTIRE PREFECTURE'S GAIN...

SO TH' OKUYODO SKYLINE GONNA BE LINKIN' UP T'THIS ROUTE 323.

'N PART O' THIS NEW ROAD'S COURSE GONNA BE ENTERIN' YER PROPERTY.

TH' PREFECTURAL GOVERNOR'S APPROVAL BE ALL BUT SECURE ...

WE'D 'PRECIATE YER COOPERATION, FER YODOYAMA'S FUTURE ...

FIRST OFF BE THIS CORNER O' YER WESTERN FIELDS.

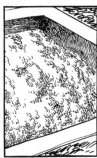

NOTE: ONE TSUBO IS ABOUT 3.3 SQUARE METERS, OR 36 SQUARE FEET.

THAT MAN SEEMS A BIT PARANOID.

BUT EITHER WAY, IT'LL END UP CUTTING ACROSS THIS FAMILY'S PROPERTY.

LANDOWNERS BE SITTIN' ON THEIR LAND WAITIN' FER PRICES T'RISE. DOWNRIVER, THEY'VE GONE UP 3,000 YEN JUST THIS PAST YEAR.

HE'S JUST TAKIN' ADVANTAGE O' US.

I SUPPOSE WE CAN REDO THE PLANS AND REROUTE THE ROAD ...

WHAT ABOUT HERE? WE'VE ALREADY NEGOTIATED HERE AND HERE, SO HE REALLY SHOULDN'T OBJECT T'THIS.

THAT LOOKS T'BE PART O' TH' PREMISES.

THERE.

AYAKO, LISTEN... NO MATTER WHAT KIND O' UPROAR ENSUES, YA JUST HANG REAL TIGHT, ALL RIGHT?

YEAH, GOOD, HIDE INSIDE THAT BLANKET! MAKE SURE NO ONE CATCHES SIGHT O' YA.

SHIRO! THEM TRUCKS HAVE SHOWN UP.

DON' LET A SINGLE ONE IN. BLOCK 'EM WIT' YER BODY!

T'HELL WIT' FORCIBLE APPRO- PRIATION!

IF THEY DARE GET NEAR TH' CELLAR, I'LL SLAUGHTER 'EM ALL!

BRO, YA CAN' DO THAT... THEY AIN' STOPPABLE.

427

GO
!

GET
'EM
!

YOU'RE UNDER ARREST FOR OB-STRUCTING PUBLIC WORK!

WH-WH WHAT DO YA THINK YA BE DOING?!

YIKES, PO-PO!

DAMMIT! TH' STOREHOUSE, I AIN' LETTIN' YA TEAR DOWN DAT S-STOREHOUSE!

SHIRO, WATCH OUT !

429

BRO, WE NEED THE YOUNG FOLKS' HELP!

ALL T'TH' BACK ROOM O' TH' MAIN HOUSE.

THESE BE TH' DEAD BIG MASTA'S LONG-CHEST. WAY OLD-FASHIONED.

ACK, WHAT TERRIBLE DUST.

YO.

THIS CHEST'S TH' LAST O' IT.

OKAY, GO AHEAD.

COMMENCE OPERATION!

430

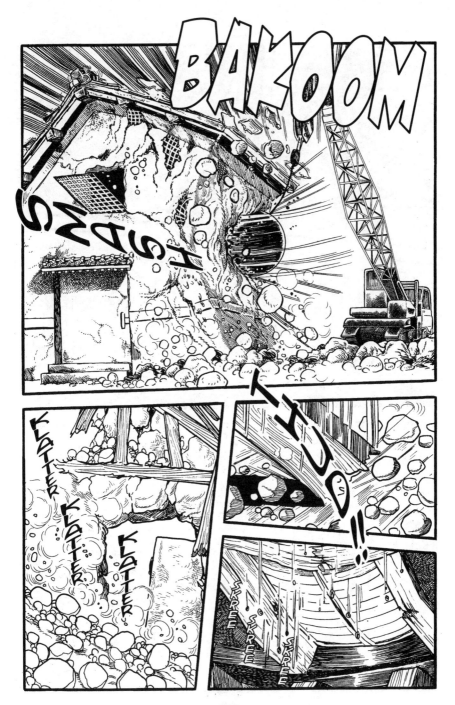

CLIK

AYAKO
...

IT BE ALL RIGHT, NOW. YA AIN' HAVE T'BE SCARED NO MORE.

I'M OPEN- IN' TH' LID.

HAVE YA FERGOTTEN? THAT THERE BE YER MA.

WELL... YER MA-IN-LAW, I SUPPOSE...

HUH. TOO MANY YEARS O' NOT SEEIN' EACH OTHER, PLUS MA'S THOROUGHLY AGED, TOO...

MA, PLEASE DON' PEEK! AYAKO BE FEARFUL O' EVERYONE OTHER THAN ME.

BUT AYAKO STILL BE PA'S CHILD... 'N NOW THAT PA'S GONE, I FEEL I OUGHTA AT LEAST LOOK AFTER HER.

IT AIN' NEEDED !! GO AWAY !!

BESIDES WHICH, THIS ALL BE TH' FRUIT O' YA BEIN' TOO WEAK-WILLED T'SPEAK OUT AGAINST WHAT PA 'N BRO WERE DOIN'!

YEAH, THAT BE TRUE, THAT BE TRUE.

I—I WANTED T'GIVE THIS T'HER. SHE OUGHTA HAVE IT.

SHIRO... PLEASE... I BEG YA, THIS BE YER MA'S ONE 'N ONLY WISH.

THAT BE AYAKO'S BANK PASSBOOK.

435

AS I THINK YA ALREADY KNOW, SOON AFTER AYAKO WAS PUT IN TH' CELLAR, MONEY IN TH' AMOUNT O' 500,000 YEN ARRIVED IN AYAKO'S NAME.

'N SINCE THEN, TOO, EVERY FEW MONTHS MONEY GETS SENT T'US, ALWAYS IN AYAKO'S NAME. I'VE SIGNED FER 'N DEPOSITED EACH 'N EVERY ONE.

THE SENDER'S NAME BE UNFAMILIAR, BUT I KNOW EXACTLY WHO IT BE. IT BE JIRO.

JIRO BEEN STASHIN' MONEY AWAY FER AYAKO.

JIRO BIG BRO ?!

HE'S STILL BEEN SENDIN' MONEY ?

SEE. THERE BE NEAR 50 MILLION YEN IN THERE NOW. THAT ALL BE AYAKO'S FORTUNE.

THIS MUCH NEITHER ICHIRO NOR YER PA KNEW NAUGHT 'BOUT.

...

I BEEN LOOKIN' SO, SO FORWARD T'THIS DAY...

AYAKO BEEN SHUT AWAY **23** YEARS, UNABLE T'GO T'SCHOOL O' GO PLAY...

I'M HOPIN' THAT MONEY CAN HELP MAKE AMENDS, 'N ATONE FER...

O-OUR HAVIN' WASTED SO MUCH O' HER LIFE.

SHE CAN USE THAT MONEY HOWEV'R WHICH WAY SHE PLEASES.

'N HERE BE TH' SENDER'S NAME 'N INFERMATION.

4-10 TSUKIJI, CHUO WARD, TOKYO... TOMIO YUTENJI.

MA.

MA!

AYAKO!

THIS BE A PASSBOOK. 'N THIS ALL BE YER MONEY.

ER, MONEY... MONEY BE...

GUESS YA DON'T KNOW!

IF YA GOT MONEY, YA CAN RULE TH' WORLD... SO YER NOW MISS BOURGEOIS! YA CAN GO T'ANY SCHOOL YA WANT! EVEN GET A COLLEGE EDUCATION.

WIT' THIS MONEY... WE CAN START YER LIFE OVER TOMORROW, AYAKO!

...

WE'LL RE-REGISTER YA... THEN WE'LL ENROLL YA IN GRADE SCHOOL.

YA CAN LEAVE IT ALL T'ME.

NAW!!

WHY NOT?

I'M NOT GOING ANY-WHERE!!

I WANNA GO BACK TO THAT CELLAR ROOM! THAT PLACE IS AYAKO'S HOME!

BUT IT DON' EXIST NO MORE. IT BEEN DEMOLISHED.

NO, NO, NO! AYAKO HAS NO PLACE TO LIVE?! WHERE AM I GONNA STAY?

I'M GONNA BUILD A GRAND NEW ROOM JUST FER YA!

438

KLATTER

MA!! I'M SO SORRY 'BOUT EARLIER...!

...

WHOOO

WHOO

OH!

OH NO, AYAKO'S GONE!

443

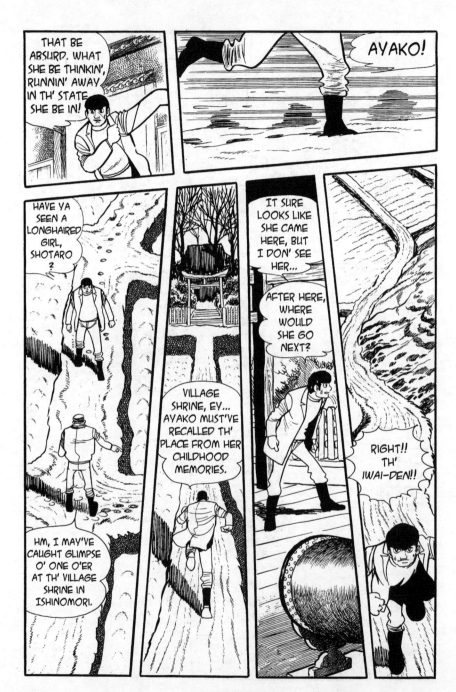

IF SHE BE WALKIN' DOWN MEMORY LANE, SHE'D THINK O' HIDIN'...

RIGHT IN THERE!!

AYAKO HID IN THAT IWAI-DEN WIT' O-RYO ONCE BEFORE.

BAM

AAH!!

I CAN' KEEP ON DOIN' THIS ALONE.

AH, THERE BE ICHIRO BIG BRO!

BRO, THEY JUST RELEASED YA?

YA SPINELESS TRAITOR!!

449

SHE BEEN MISSIN' SINCE THIS MORNIN', 'N WE BEEN SCURRYIN' 'BOUT.

SO IT SEEMS AYAKO MAY'VE TAKEN OFF WIT' MISS SU'E'S KIMONO?

PUTTIN' THAT ASIDE FER NOW ...

CARE T'EXPLAIN THIS, ICHIRO?

MISS SU'E'S BANK PASSBOOK, SEAL, PURSE, JEWELRY, EVEN HER PERSONAL EFFECTS, TH' WHOLE LOT.

THEY WERE ALL SHOVED INSIDE TH' CHEST.

WHY'D MISS SU'E LEAVE ALL THESE BEHIND WHEN SHE'D UP 'N LEFT HERE?

THAT'S MIGHTY FOOLISH, ESPECIALLY FER THAT METICULOUS GIRL.

ICHIRO!! DID SU'E REALLY UP 'N LEAVE?

WHERE SHE BE RIGHT NOW?!

453

CHAPTER 16

THE OUSHINKAI

MUTSU SHIPPING? WE DON'T DO ANY BUSINESS WITH 'EM.

YES... THIS IS T.K. ENTERPRISES.

OUR CHAIRMAN? TOMIO YUTENJI.

YUTENJI... YANKEE, UNCLE, TANGO, EASY, NANCY, JAM, INDIA.

HELLO? THIS IS SENIOR DIRECTOR KINJO. HOW MAY I HELP YOU? HUH? A WOMAN? HOLDIN' AN ENVELOPE BEARIN' OUR CHAIRMAN'S NAME?

A WOMAN, DIRECTOR?

NOT SOME LADY FRIEND. THEY SAY SHE WAS A STOWAWAY ON A TRUCK.

THE POLICE HAVE HER IN THEIR CARE, BUT BOSS GOTTA VOUCH FOR HER.

GO, GO TO THE POLICE AND BRING HER HERE.

ME? I'D RATHER NOT, SIR.

AT LEAST ONE COPPER WILL KNOW WHO I AM.

I'LL CALL BOSS. HE WENT GOLFIN' YESTERDAY. HE MUST STILL BE IN BED.

HI, IT'S KINJO. ACTUALLY, A GIRL WHO RAN AWAY FROM HOME IS ASKIN' FOR YOU.

GIRL? ONE JUST LEFT. I'M SLEEPING IN TODAY, SO DON'T DISTURB ME.

WHAT? QUIT JOKING AROUND, KINJO.

I DON'T CARE FOR COUNTRY BUMPKINS!

HM?

MM.

HMM.

A TRUCK THAT ORIGINATED IN YODOYAMA?

SHE WAS HIDING INSIDE IT? WHAT DOES SHE LOOK LIKE? DOES SHE HAVE ANY I.D. ON HER?

ALL RIGHT!! SOMEONE GO PICK HER UP AND BRING HER STRAIGHT HERE.

I AM THE SENDER OF THE ENVELOPE YOU WERE CARRYING, TOMIO YUTENJI HIMSELF.

KRI

KRIIIIK

KLOMP

ARE SHIRO AND MA WELL?

I KNOW YOUR FAMILY FINE, YOU SEE.

YOUR OLD FRIEND O-RYO, TOO.

SHE DIED, DIDN'T SHE, THE POOR THING... BUT IT MUST HAVE BEEN EVEN HARDER FOR YOU.

IMPRISONED AND FORCED TO LIVE INSIDE A STOREHOUSE FOR 23 YEARS...

YOU WOULDN'T KNOW, BUT THE OTHER DAY, A MAN WHO'D SURVIVED IN THE JUNGLE FOR 27 YEARS CAME HOME TO JAPAN... YOUR SITUATIONS ARE SIMILAR.

YOU DON'T HAVE TO COME NEAR... JUST STAND THERE AND LET ME GAZE UPON YOU FOR A WHILE...

MAKE YOURSELF AT HOME.

I'LL HAVE THEM ROUND UP SOME CLOTHES AND THINGS. MY HOUSEKEEPER IS REAL SWEET.

TAKE CARE OF THAT CHILD. JUST...

DON'T LOOK AT HER STRAIGHT IN THE FACE, AND DON'T SPEAK TO HER.

I'LL ACT AS INTERMEDIARY BETWEEN US!

SHE IS MINE ALONE!!

...

...

HE WAS CRYING, WASN'T HE?

IT'S THE FIRST TIME I'VE EVER SEEN TEARS ON HIS FACE.

467

THE POLITICOS' MAINTENANCE COSTS HAVE INCREASED ABOUT 15% COMPARED TO LAST TERM.

WHY?

ENTERTAINMENT EXPENSES. AKASAKA DISTRICT'S GOTTEN PRICEY.

PLUS, THE CONTRIBUTION TO MISTER YANAGIDA IS QUITE SUBSTANTIAL.

BOSS, I'M GONNA BE FRANK WITH YOU, SO PLEASE HEAR ME OUT WITHOUT LOSIN' IT, OKAY?

SURE, GO AHEAD, KINJO.

BOSS, I REALLY WISH YOU'D LIMIT YOUR ASSOCIATIN' WITH POLITICOS TO A MINIMUM...

THERE'S NO END TO IT.

THESE POLITICOS, NO MATTER HOW MUCH MONEY YOU LAVISH ON 'EM...

HOW HELPFUL WILL THEY REALLY BE IN A PINCH?

...

THEY'RE COLD CREATURES...

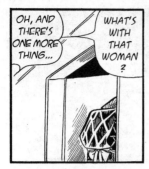

NOTE: THE PHRASE "GIRL IN A BOX" REFERS TO A SHELTERED GIRL OR DAUGHTER.

YOU LOOK ...

SO LIKE YOUR MO— THER...

I BELIEVE YOU HAVE A MOLE ON YOUR NECK?

YOUR MOTHER HAD ONE... YOU KNOW WHO I MEAN?

SIS—IN— LAW, SU'E.

SHE PRE— TENDED TO BE YOUR SISTER, BUT SHE'S YOUR MOTHER.

WHO'RE YOU?

BREAKFAST?

YOU CAN EAT WHATEVER DELICIOUS THINGS YOU WANT FROM NOW ON.

MAKE HER SOME SOUP.

YARDS THAT GET THIS MANY SONGBIRDS ARE RARE IN TOKYO.

WE FEED THEM EVERY DAY, SO THEY NEVER LEAVE, SINCE THEY CAN EAT THEIR FILL.

YOU DON'T PUT THEM IN CAGES?

I HATE CAGES.

SEEING PET BIRDS IN A CAGE WITHOUT EVER FLYING THEIR ENTIRE LIVES IRKS ME.

HOW YOU WERE DOING IN THAT CELLAR EVERY DAY, THESE PAST 20-ODD YEARS, HAUNTED ME IN MY DREAMS.

WHY?

WHO ARE YOU? TELL ME!

EVERYTHING WITHIN THESE WALLS IS YOURS TO USE AS YOU PLEASE.

BROOM

YOU'RE CONNECTED, MR. YUTENJI, AND EXTENSIVELY INVOLVED IN VARIOUS BUSINESSES. I'D LOVE TO HAVE SOME OF YOUR CRUMBS.

OH, PLEASE ...

FOLKS LIKE ME WHO'VE RELIED ON CYCLE RACING...

ARE IN A SORT OF COMA THANKS TO THE GAMBLING BAN.

CAN'T NO LONGER MAKE A LIVELI-HOOD OUT OF THE HOSTESS BIZ OR FROM EASY MONEY.

WE CAN USE THIS OPPORTUNITY TO MAKE PEACE WITH EACH OTHER AND JOIN FORCES...

I'D LIKE THAT VERY MUCH INDEED.

YOU HAVE A CALL, SIR.

KIN-JO.

WHAT ?!

3 OF ICHOUKAI'S MID-LEVEL BRASS WERE ATTACKED AT CLUB MEMORY. ONE IS DEAD AND THE OTHER 2 ARE GRAVELY WOUNDED.

ONE OF OUR GUYS THE ATTACKER?

IT AIN'T CLEAR. THE SHOOTER RAN OFF. I DON'T THINK IT'S ONE OF US. THE WHOLE THING WAS DUE TO SOME TRIVIAL ARGUMENT.

I'LL BE RIGHT THERE!

I CAN'T BELIEVE THIS MESS IS HAPPENING RIGHT NOW!

WHAT?!

EVERYONE KNOWS THAT THE OUSHINKAI AND ICHOUKAI ARE ONE SPARK AWAY FROM WAR.

IN FACT, ISN'T THAT WHY YOU MET UP WITH MORIDEN TONIGHT?

BUT "THE CHILD KNOWS NOT HIS PARENT'S HEART," HUH?

CONSIDERING THE SIMPLISTIC MOTIVE, I BET IT WAS ONE OF YOUR HOODLUMS.

ENEMY BRASS ACT BIG AT YOUR CLUB, DRUNKEN HOODLUM BLOWS A FUSE.

IF WE HAVE ANY SUCH FELLOW, HE'LL BE DRAGGED OUT AND TAUGHT A LESSON.

WE SHAN'T PERMIT SUCH A THING.

HARD TO BELIEVE THAT JIRO TENGE, PARTY IF ONLY MENIALLY TO THE ASSASSINATION ORGAN OF THE CANON UNIT 20-PLUS YEARS AGO, WOULD GET FLUSTERED BY THE ACTIONS OF A HOODLUM.

SHUT UP!

YOU'VE LOST YOUR EDGE, MISTER TENGE.

479

480

BLAM!!

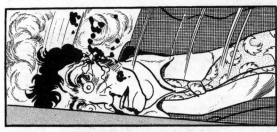

PUT THIS IN HIS HAND.

I'M GOING HOME TO THINK UP COUNTER-MEASURES.

HANDLE GETA FOR ME, KINJO.

THAT WAS UNFORTUNATE.

IF WE'D ONLY BEEN FASTER WITH THE I.D.,

INOUE WOULD STILL BE ALIVE...

FATHER, WHY DO YOU KEEP CALLING YUTENJI BY THE NAME "TENGE"?

OH, HIM?

BECAUSE HIS REAL NAME IS TENGE...

MY MENTOR MISTER TANUMA HAD BEEN CHASING HIM.

IT WAS AROUND THE TIME OF THE SHIMOKAWA INCIDENT, 1949, I THINK...

HE WAS INVOLVED IN A MURDER.

EVIDENCE GATHERING TOOK TOO LONG, AND HE GOT AWAY.

AND MISTER TANUMA SUCCUMBED TO CANCER...

YOU PROBABLY DON'T REMEMBER THE TIME MISTER TANUMA CAME TO OUR HOUSE AND GAVE YOU A SOUVENIR, WHEN YOU WERE LITTLE.

MM, NO, I DON'T.

ON HIS DEATHBED, MISTER TANUMA BESEECHED ME...

TO "PLEASE TRACK DOWN AND NAB TENGE SOME DAY"!

HE WAS A TENACIOUS MAN...

I GOT MY DOGGEDNESS FROM HIM, YOU KNOW.

WELL, I'M OFF TO THE PUBLIC PROSECUTOR'S OFFICE.

SURE...

HE'S BECOME A FINE BUDDING PROSECUTOR...

HE WAS SO SKINNY BACK THEN, AFTER THE WAR.

T.K. ENTERPRISES CO.
GINZA OFFICE

BE THERE SOMEONE HERE BY TH' NAME O' TOMIO YUTENJI?

OUR CHAIRMAN, YOUR BUSINESS?

CHAIRMAN?

UH... ER...

TELL HIM I WANT T'TALK T'HIM 'BOUT AYAKO.

AYAKO? A WOMAN?

AND WHAT IS THIS IN REGARDS TO?

I'M PRETTY SURE AYAKO BE HERE!

WHAT DID YOU SAY YOUR NAME WAS? THIS IS T.K. ENTERPRISES...

THIS MAN YUTENJI'S BEEN SENDIN' MONEY T'AYAKO EVERY MONTH... 'N SHE RAN AWAY FROM HOME 2 DAYS AGO. I ASSUMED SHE'D COME HERE...

HEY, HELP ME OUT HERE. I DON'T KNOW WHAT TO SAY.

WHAT'S YOUR BUSINESS?

THAT BE WHAT I BEEN TRYIN' T'TELL YA!

I WANNA TALK T'THIS YUTENJI FELLA!!

487

488

MY WORD ... SHIRO!

COME ON IN, WHAT BRINGS YOU HERE?

HEHEH... I'M PRETTY GOOD AT FINDIN' PLACES, EY.

I'D HEARD YA'D MOVED T'KAWASAKI, 'N SINCE I'D COME DOWN T'TOKYO...

YER HUSBAND OUT?

OF COURSE. HE'S AT THE FACTORY.

YA'VE GOT A NICE PLACE, SIS.

IT BE REAL DEPRESSIN' AT HOME...

HOW'S IT BEEN, SINCE...?

EVEN GLOOM- IER.

A MURK THAT CAN' BE HELPED.

THE TENGE FAMILY IS DONE FOR.

AYAKO LEFT TH' CELLAR 'N RAN AWAY.

WHAT?!

WHERE TO?

TOKYO... T'THIS YUTENJI FELLA'S PLACE.

WHEN I GOT THERE, THEY BOOTED ME... TOKYO BE A HORRIBLE PLACE!!

WHO'S YUTENJI?

BOTH MA 'N I THINK...

HE BE JIRO BIG BRO.

JIRO?

AYAKO GOT SICK O' TH' MOOD IN OUR HOUSE, 'N RAN AWAY... 'N WHERE'D SHE GO? SHE SNUCK ABOARD A MUTSU SHIPPIN' TRUCK 'N CAME HERE T'TOKYO, 'N GOT TAKEN T'YUTENJI'S OFFICE. THAT BE TH' FARTHEST I'VE MANAGED T'GET.

HE BEEN SENDIN' THOUSANDS O' YEN T'AYAKO

...EVERY FEW MONTHS. TH' ONLY PERSON WHO'D KNOW HER 'N DO SUCH A THING BE HIM.

I'VE POURED YOU TEA, MISS AYAKO.

WANT TO COME OUT AND DRINK IT?

HUH?

HEYA, GEN, SHE'S MISSING.

SHE AIN'T IN THE YARD?

NO, I THINK SHE MAY HAVE GONE OUTSIDE.

GOTTA BE KIDDIN' ME. THAT WENCH WANNA GET ME IN TROUBLE?

GEN, HEY GEN!! COME HERE!

493

LOOK AT THIS! SHE MADE SUCH A BIG HOLE!

WHY NOT WALK STRAIGHT OUT THE FRONT DOOR?

I BET SHE SAW YOU STANDING GUARD THERE AND GOT FRIGHTENED.

EVEN THOUGH I GOT A KINDLY MUG THAT WOMEN LOVE?

THAT CHILD JUST HATES PEOPLE... SHE'S ALWAYS SO JUMPY.

WHAT'S THE MOST REMOTE, NON-BUSTLING PLACE AROUND HERE?

INSIDE THE PUBLIC TOILETS.

SILLY.

...

494

GIGGLE

495

TEE HEE, YOU SUCK.

WANNA PLAY HOP-SCOTCH, BIG SIS?

SURE, LET'S!!

HAVEN'T SEEN HER AROUND BEFORE.

WHAT LEISURE, TO HAVE TIME TO PLAY WITH KIDS.

OH HO HO... HO HO HO...

HERE, TAKE THIS.

ARE YOU MISTER YUTENJI'S YOUNG LADY?

WHAT ARE YOU SO JUMPY FOR?

...

I'M NOT A COP. AH, WHERE ARE MY MANNERS. I SHOULD INTRODUCE MYSELF FIRST.

MY NAME IS HANAO GETA. I WORK AT THE PROSECUTOR'S OFFICE.

I CAME HERE TO CHECK OUT MISTER YUTENJI'S RESIDENCE...

SINCE MY DAD'S LINKED TO HIM.

I'M AYAKO, I...

I'M JUST STAYING HERE...

OH, OKAY! GOOD!

WHY?

I'M GLAD YOU'RE NOT THE DAUGHTER OF A MOB BOSS...

HEY, THE OUSHINKAI'S HERE!!

THEY CAME? HOW MANY? DAMMIT!

HEY, Y'ALL!

JUST ONE.

ONE? THEY'RE DISRE-SPECTIN' US!!

IT'S THEIR CHAIRMAN, YUTENJI'S HERE!

ALONE? SERIOUSLY? THIS OUGHT TO BE INTERESTIN'.

YUTENJI CAME ALONE? HMPH, I WONDER WHAT HE'S PLOTTIN'. MAYBE HE'S STUPID?

PTOO

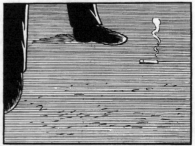

I WANT TO SEE YOUR CHAIRMAN.

HEH, THIS DOOR AIN'T BUDGIN' FOR YA, UNLESS YA PAY UP.

IT AIN'T OPENIN' UNTIL YA BRING AT LEAST 3 OUSHINKAI BRASS.

THAT'S WHAT OUR BOSS IS EXPECTIN', TOO.

WHY'D YA COME ALONE?

TO TALK TO HIM. WHY BRING OTHERS?

BE SERIOUS!

THE MAN RESPONSIBLE FOR YOUR BRASS'S DEATHS, INOUE, KILLED HIMSELF. THE COPS ARE INVESTIGATING IT RIGHT NOW.

I WANT TO CLEAR THE AIR WITH YOUR CHAIRMAN BEFORE IT'S TOO LATE.

YOU'RE A SCOUNDREL WHO AIN'T KNOW A THING ABOUT THE CODE!

EVEN IF OUR BOSS DECIDES TO FORGIVE YA, WE SHAN'T.

EVEN IF YA GOT ON YOUR KNEES.

WH-WH-WHAT'S UP W-WITH THAT EYE?!

YOU'VE READ ABOUT LETTER BOMBS IN THE PAPERS, HAVEN'T YOU?

SO LONG AS YOU'VE GOT A TRIGGERING DEVICE, YOU CAN EVEN SET A BOMB INSIDE A MINIATURE LIGHT BULB.

ALTHOUGH THIS IS SPECIAL ORDER.

BRAND-NEW MODEL USED BY AMERICAN INTELLIGENCE.

THEY DEVELOPED IT FOR IMPLANTING IN CUFF-LINKS.

IF I FALL DOWN, AND THE PRO-TRUDING BIT HITS THE GROUND...

BOOM... THE BLAST RADIUS IS ABOUT 30 METERS.

DON'T FOR-GET IT.

...

UNNH...

I'LL SAY THIS JUST ONCE MORE. YOU HOOLIGANS GET LOST. I WANT TO SEE CHAIRMAN MORIDEN.

...YES, SIR.

P-PLEASE COME IN.

MISTER YUTENJI, I'M IN NO MOOD TO LISTEN TO EXCUSES AT THIS POINT.

FIRST, PLEASE ACCEPT THIS GIFT.

WE CEDE TO ICHOUKAI THE RIGHTS TO 3RD AND 4TH STREETS OF SASAHAMA BLOCK... THIS ISN'T GOING TO CUT IT.

THAT WAS JUST A GIFT.

MAY I MAKE A CALL?

~~ ~~

MISTER MORIDEN, PLEASE TAKE THIS.

HELLO? THIS IS IDOBATA OF THE NATIONAL LAND RESTRUCTURING AND DEVELOPMENT AGENCY.

THE DIRECTOR-GENERAL HIMSELF!

PARTY POLICY CHIEF YANAGIDA SPOKE TO ME...

YOU'RE A FRIEND OF MISTER YUTENJI'S?

ER... YES.

YUTENJI MAY BE YOUNG, BUT WELL, PLEASE BE OF HELP TO HIM.

SORRY TO DO THIS OVER THE PHONE, BUT COULD I GET YOUR ADVICE?

ABOUT THE MAINLAND-YOMOJIMA BRIDGE PROJECT.

I'D LIKE YOU TO HANDLE THE PUBLIC WORKS...

THAT'S THE GIST OF IT. THE BUDGET IS STILL UNDER NEGOTIATION, BUT IT'LL BE ACTUALIZED WITHIN THIS FISCAL TERM.

IF YOU'RE WILLING TO TAKE THIS ON, COULD YOU SET ASIDE SOME TIME OVER THE NEXT SEVERAL DAYS FOR US TO MEET?

W-WELL, THIS IS SUCH A SUDDEN OFFER, M-MAY I HAVE A LITTLE TIME TO THINK IT OVER...

A-A-AND GET BACK TO YOU?

Y-YES, YOU ARE QUITE RIGHT.

YES, THANK YOU VERY MUCH.

KACHING

SIGH

PLEASE TAKE THE OFFER. IT'LL GET YOU AROUND 3 BILLION YEN IN PROFIT.

WHOA

TH-THREE BILLION?

PLUS, MISTER IDOBATA IS CLOSE TO THE PRIME MINISTER...

IT WON'T HURT FOR YOU TO KNOW HIM, HA HA HA...

HEH HEH HEH...

HE'S LEAVING. SEE HIM OFF!

VROOM

BOSS... WHAT HAPPENED?

MESSIN' WITH HIM WOULD BE A MISTAKE. I CAN USE HIS BACKDOOR CONNECTIONS.

HE HAS NO IDEA IDOBATA IS A DEAD-ENDER. WHAT A POLITICAL INNOCENT, HO HO...

CHAPTER 17

THE SILK TREE BLOSSOM

23 YEARS ?!

YOU WERE IMPRISONED INSIDE A CELLAR FOR 23 YEARS AND JUST GAINED YOUR FREEDOM? WHAT A DREADFUL LIFE!!

YOU OUGHT TO FILE CHARGES AGAINST THEM FOR THAT!

GET REPARATIONS! AT THE TRIALS OF POLLUTION VICTIMS AND OTHER MAJOR CASES...

... SORRY... TRIALS AND POLLUTION SICKNESS ARE MEANINGLESS TO YOU, AREN'T THEY.

SO, WHAT NOW?

ARE YOU GOING TO FORGIVE YOUR FAMILY?

I DON'T KNOW. I DON'T KNOW WHAT TO DO...

WHY BE SO ATTACHED TO A MOB BOSS'S HOUSE?!

AM I... A CHILD?

I USED TO PLAY WITH A WOMAN NAMED O-RYO. I REMEMBER IT CLEARLY. WE'D HOP AROUND ON ONE FOOT, OR JUMP ROPE. BUT EVERYONE WHO WAS WATCHING US WOULD LAUGH HARD!

YOU'RE 27. THAT MAKES YOU A FINE ADULT.

WHEN I PLAYED, THEY ALL LAUGHED AT ME.

MY HUSBAND'S STUCK AT WORK... FEEL FREE TO STAY A WHILE.

I'D LIKE YOU TO MEET HIM.

THANKS, BUT I'LL HAVE T'PASS FER TODAY.

HE BE A GOOD MAN?

YES, VERY GOOD.

SORRY T'BRING THIS UP, BUT HAVE YA FORGOTTEN 'BOUT YER OLD LOVER YET?

I'LL NEVER FORGET THAT MAN.

NOT ONLY HAVEN'T I FORGOTTEN ABOUT HIM...

I CAN STILL CLEARLY PICTURE MR. ENO THOUGH IT'S BEEN **20** YEARS.

I DREAM ABOUT HIM SEVERAL TIMES A MONTH.

HE JUST STARES AT ME...

AS IF HE WANTS TO SAY SOMETHING. IT'S SO HEARTBREAKING.

SHIRO, I HAVE NEVER ONCE STOPPED THINKING ABOUT AVENGING HIS DEATH.

CASES FROM BACK THEN ARE GETTING RESOLVED ONLY NOW.

THE INDICTED ARE BEING ACQUITTED AND RELEASED, AND I DOUBT THE VICTIMS ARE SATISFIED.

THE TRUE PERPS ARE STILL AT LARGE!

I BET THEY'RE REAL VEXED.

THE YODOYAMA INCIDENT'S STILL IN A MIRE. THE INSPECTOR IN CHARGE PASSED AWAY.

NO ONE'S GOTTEN TO THE BOTTOM OF'T...

BUT I'LL NEVER FORGET!

I SWEAR ...

ONE DAY, I'LL UNMASK THE TRUTH AND DRAG FORTH THE ONES WHO KILLED HIM...

FOR THE WHOLE WORLD TO SEE, SO HE CAN REST IN PEACE.

THAT'S MY DREAM. HO HO HO...

TENGU

NO MATTER HOW MUCH THE WORLD CHANGES...

GRUDGES SHAN'T EVER FADE.

SIS... YA NEVER THOUGHT JIRO BRO COULD BE TH' CULPRIT?

YOU KNOW, YOU'VE MENTIONED THAT TO ME ONCE BEFORE...

JIRO ISN'T CAPABLE OF SUCH A THING.

IT WAS THEM AMERICANS THAT KILLED HIM!

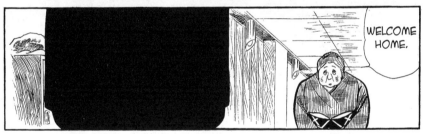

WELCOME HOME.

I'M SO TIRED...

IS AYAKO ASLEEP?

MASTER, IT'S ABOUT MISS AYAKO.

EVERY DAY, SHE SNEAKS OUTSIDE AND SCATTERS MONEY AROUND THE NEIGHBORHOOD.

MONEY?

YES. TODAY, SHE GAVE 10,000 YEN NOTES TO CHILDREN IN THE PARK.

SHE DID?

YES, WE'VE RECEIVED NUMEROUS COMPLAINTS FROM THEIR PARENTS.

SOME ARE ADVISING US THAT SHE'S MENTALLY ILL AND OUGHT TO BE HOSPITALIZED.

AYAKO STILL DOESN'T KNOW WHAT MONEY IS. SHE'S VERY SPECIAL.

BUT THIS IS JUST TOO MUCH, SIR.

LEAVE HER ALONE.

I ABSOLUTELY FORBID YOU TO SCOLD AYAKO ABOUT ANYTHING.

I'LL TEACH HER, EVENTUALLY.

THAT MONEY SHE'S GIVING OUT IS HERS. SHE CAN USE IT AS SHE PLEASES.

OH DEAR.

EVEN MASTER HAS GOTTEN ODD.

523

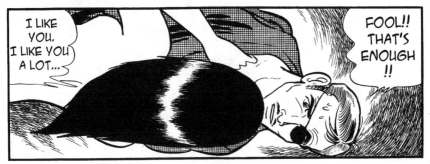

KLOMP

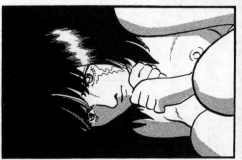

THE POOR THING...

AND IT'S MY FAULT SHE'S LIKE THAT.

I HAVE NO RIGHT TO SCOLD YOU, AYAKO!!

TO UNTWIST YOUR WARPED SENSE...

TO RESTORE YOU IS THE LEAST I CAN DO TO ATONE.

WHETHER IT TAKES YEARS OR DECADES, I'LL DO RIGHT BY YOU.

IF IT TAKES THE REST OF MY LIFE.

FATHER, CAN I TALK TO YOU?

IT'S ABOUT MO- THER.

HOW DID YOU AND MOTHER END UP TOGETHER, AGAIN?

NOW THAT'S UNEX- PECTED.

MOTHER NEVER WENT INSIDE THE MPD STATION...

BECAUSE SHE DESPISED POLICE AUTHORITY, RIGHT?

SHE WAS IN PRISON, LONG AGO.

... FOR LÈSE MAJ- ESTÉ.

FOR SLANDERING THE ARMED FORCES DURING THE WAR.

YEAH... THAT'S RIGHT. SHE WAS THROWN IN PRISON FOR IDEOLOGICAL INFRACTION.

AFTER THE WAR, POLITICAL PRISONERS WERE PARDONED AND SHE WAS RELEASED. SHE WAS QUITE DESPONDENT ABOUT HER FUTURE.

THE ONE WHO GENTLY BOLSTERED YOUR MA BACK THEN WAS MY MENTOR INSPECTOR TANUMA.

AND ONE DAY, HE INTRODUCED HER TO ME, A ROOKIE COP AT THE TIME.

IT WAS LOVE AT FIRST SIGHT.

LOVE AT FIRST SIGHT, HUH.

YEAH. I DIDN'T CARE A WHIT ABOUT HER PAST.

YOU DON'T THINK YOU ACTED OUT OF A SUBCONSCIOUS PITY FOR HER?

THAT'S WHAT I WANTED TO ASK YOU. YOU DIDN'T MARRY HER OUT OF SYMPATHY?

SYMPATHY? RIDICULOUS.

NO. I REALLY FELL IN LOVE WITH HER.

531

SUBCONSCIOUS? PERHAPS. BUT PERHAPS NOT. NONE OF THAT MATTERED TO ME BACK THEN, ANYWAY.

WHY ARE YOU ASKING ME THIS, NOW?

IS LOVE THAT ARISES FROM PITY, UNTRUE?

THESE THINGS ARE EXAM TOPICS?

NO... JUST SEEKING PERSONAL ADVICE.

FOR WHOM?

HANAO... ARE YOU IN LOVE?

I'M NOT SURE... THAT'S WHY I WANTED TO ASK YOUR OPINION.

SO YOU CAN'T EVEN TELL IF WHAT YOU'RE FEELING IS PITY OR LOVE.

YOU SAID IT.

YOU'RE A BOOR LIKE ME... YOU CAN'T SOUND OUT THE GIRL'S FEELINGS, CAN YOU?

WE'VE GOTTEN FULLY PHYSICAL ALREADY.

WHAT?!

WHEN DID YOU START DATING?

WE JUST MET TODAY.

BY THE...

I'M SHOCKED SPEECHLESS!!

'NIGHT, FATHER.

...

AYAKO...

DON'T YOU START TALKING BIG!!

DOES IT PAIN YOU THAT MUCH

THAT I RESOLVED THINGS WITH MORIDEN MY OWN WAY ?!

LET ME MAKE THIS CLEAR. OUSHINKAI IS WHERE IT IS NOW BECAUSE I GOT ASSEMBLYMEN AND CONGLOMERATES IN OUR CORNER, POLITICALLY!

IT WASN'T THANKS TO BRUTE FORCE!

MORIDEN'S FAMILY HAS HELD SWAY FOR SOME TIME.

THEY'D BEAT US IN A WAR. MORE THAN A FEW BOSSES WOULD TAKE MORIDEN'S SIDE.

THERE, BOSS, NOW YOU'RE UNDER-RATIN' OUR LADS.

THEY DON'T UNDER-STAND A THING!

HOW WILL YOU TELL THEM YOU HANDED OVER...

TWO BLOCKS IN SASA-HAMA?

STILL MAD ABOUT LAST NIGHT? FINE. YOUR NEW OUTFIT IS READY, SO TRY IT ON.

WE'RE HEADING OUT.

WE'LL DO A LITTLE TOKYO SIGHTSEEING.

WHY DID YOU COME HERE?

THIS PLACE IS TOO ROUGH FOR YOU.

WELL? ISN'T IT SUCH A DIRTY SKY? AND THE AIR SMELLY? 10 MILLION PEOPLE LIVE HERE, ALL CRAMMED INTO THIS SPACE.

SOMEONE DIES EVERY FEW MINUTES... PEOPLE AREN'T TREATED LIKE PEOPLE HERE. IT'S A CITY OF FOOLS WHO'RE PRETTY SATISFIED WITH THEIR LOT REGARDLESS.

YOU'D BE BETTER OFF IN YODO-YAMA...

NOW THAT YOU'RE FREE.

PA'S DEAD...

WEREN'T SHIRO AND MA LOOKING OUT FOR YOU?

WHO ARE YOU?

TELL ME, WHO?

A MAN WHO DIED LONG AGO.

...

538

WHAT ARE WE GOING TO DO HERE?

WE'RE GOING TO REST FOR A WHILE, AND THEN EAT DINNER.

THIS IS CALLED AN ELEVATOR...

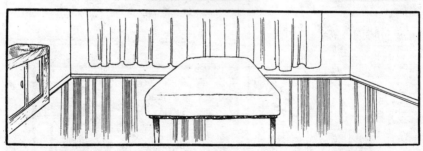

NOW MAKE YOURSELF AT HOME...

WEIRD ROOM.

LET'S PLAY A GAME, AYAKO. I'M GOING TO PUT THIS SACK OVER MY HEAD.

THEN, I'LL SPEAK IN A FUNNY VOICE. IF YOU LAUGH OR TALK BACK, YOU LOSE.

OKAY?

BE RIGHT BACK.

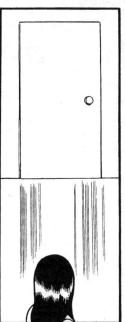

YOUR EYELIDS ...

ARE STARTING TO FEEL VERY, VERY HEAVY...

YOU'RE NOT ABLE TO KEEP THEM OPEN. SEE, YOU ARE SHUTTING YOUR EYES!

YOU'RE FALLING INTO A DEEP, DEEP SLEEP ...

YOU FEEL REALLY, REALLY GOOD RIGHT NOW...

YOU ARE GROWING YOUNGER...

YOUNGER AND YOUNGER...

SEE, YOU'RE 15 YEARS OLD AGAIN!

NOW ...

YOU ARE GETTING EVEN YOUNGER. YOU'RE A CHILD AGAIN, 10 YEARS OLD... AND STILL YOUNGER...

YOU'RE NOW 4, 4 YEARS OLD.

YOU ARE PLAYING. YOU CAN SEE YOUR FAMILY'S STOREHOUSE. YOU GO TO THE STOREHOUSE... YOU'RE STANDING IN FRONT OF IT. WILL YOU GO INSIDE? NO, YOU WILL NOT!!

YOU WILL NOT ENTER THE STOREHOUSE, UNDERSTAND?!

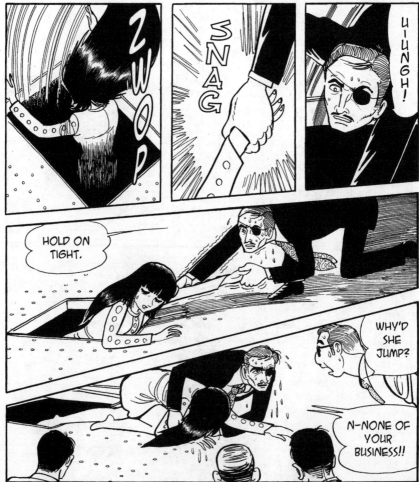

NOW, I APOLOGIZE FOR HAVING DECEIVED YOU! BUT I WISH YOU'D APPRECIATE MY TRYING TO REHABILITATE YOU!

YOU HAVE A RESERVATION? MISTER YUTENJI? AH, YES, THIS WAY, PLEASE.

I WANTED TO TAKE YOU TO A RESTAURANT... BUT GIVEN THE STATE YOU'RE IN...

YOU WERE TO BE A PARTY OF TWO?

WHO THE HECK DOES HE THINK HE IS?

YEAH, WE'RE NOT ROOM SERVICE, YOU KNOW.

THAT'S RIGHT. MY COMPANION IS STILL IN THE CAR.

I HAVE A FAVOR TO ASK. CAN I HAVE THE OTHER MEAL DELIVERED OUT TO THE CAR?

HERE IS YOUR SOUP.

A MENTALLY CHALLENGED BELLE.

DON'T GET TOO CLOSE.

WE DID BRING HER PLATES OUT TO THE CAR...

BUT SHE WILL NOT EAT.

I SEE.

THEN I APOLOGIZE, BUT MAY I BORROW AN EMPTY BOX LARGE ENOUGH FOR A PERSON TO FIT INSIDE?

STEP ASIDE, STEP ASIDE.

I AM SO SORRY, SIR, BUT WE DO NOT HAVE SUCH A ...

SUMMON THE MANAGER! I AM TOMIO YUTENJI!!

549

YOU STILL ANGRY?

YOU'RE **27** ALREADY. WOMEN GET MARRIED AT YOUR AGE.

EVEN IF YOU WERE TO MEET SOMEONE...

HE'LL RUN AWAY IF YOU REMAIN THE WAY YOU ARE.

YOU DON'T WANT TO MAKE AN EFFORT TO FIX YOURSELF?

THIS IS MY COMPANY OFFICE.

WE'RE IN THE SHOW BUSINESS. YOU'RE AS PRETTY AS OUR GIRLS...

WHAT ARE YOU LOOKING AT?

WHO IS THAT MAN?

YOU KNOW HIM? HOW?

THAT'S HANAO...

WHAT?

SO?

AYAKO AND I MET EACH OTHER IN A PARK NEAR YOUR RESIDENCE.

JUST ONCE?

WE'VE DATED A FEW TIMES ALREADY.

I'M GOING TO BE FRANK. AYAKO IS MISERABLE.

SHE REALLY SHOULDN'T BE KEPT AT YOUR HOUSE!

I'M THE ONLY ONE WHO CAN MAKE HER HAPPY.

...

YOU'RE A BIT TOO FRANK.

WHY IS IT WRONG FOR AYAKO TO STAY HERE?

DO YOU KNOW AYAKO'S BACKGROUND?

SHE TOLD ME.

I DO REALIZE THAT YOU'RE HER GUARDIAN. YOU DO HAVE LOTS OF MONEY, TOO...

BUT CAN AYAKO REALLY BECOME NORMAL THIS WAY?

AS A MOB BOSS'S MISTRESS?

WATCH YOUR MOUTH!

AND SO ...

WHAT DO YOU PROPOSE?

556

I'M SETTING A CONDITION. ACKNOWLEDGE ME AS AYAKO'S GUARDIAN. LET ME KEEP TAKING CARE OF HER.

I'LL PAY HER LIVING AND OTHER EXPENSES.

I CAN COME AND GO FREELY.

ACCEPT, AND I'LL ENTRUST AYAKO TO YOU FOR A YEAR.

JUST ONE YEAR ?!

IF, AFTER A YEAR, YOU'VE MADE HER UNHAPPY ...

I SWEAR ON MY HONOR THAT YOU'LL GET IT!

THAT'S YOUR CONDITION ?

I'LL PICK A HOUSE AND FURNISH IT IN THE NEXT FEW DAYS, SO CALL ME.

IN THE MEANTIME, DON'T YOU GO LURKING AROUND MY HOUSE!!

NOW GO ON HOME!

AND FEEL LUCKY THAT I'M LETTING YOU GO.

IS THIS A BUILT-FOR-SALE?

ONE OF MY SECONDARY HOMES. AS GOOD AS NEW.

COME LOOK INSIDE.

NICE, ISN'T IT?

LADY-KILLER, I PRAY AYAKO WON'T BE NEEDING THIS.

IT'S LIKE A COFFIN FOR THE TRUST-IMPAIRED.

MR. YUTENJI, YOU MAY BE THE FREQUENTLY BLACKLISTED HEAD OF OUSHINKAI, BUT YOU'RE NOT A BAD MAN.

YOU SURE DON'T MINCE YOUR WORDS, YOUNGSTER.

GOOD NIGHT, AYAKO.

HMPH.

BOSS!
HOW CAN YA LET
THAT URCHIN
DISRESPECT YA
LIKE THAT?!

YOU SHUT
UP AND
STAY OUT
OF THIS!!

HEH HEH... HEH HEH HEH.

DELIVERY FROM THE BOSS ... REAL TASTY FOOD, FROM SHIMBASHI.

THAT LOUT SURE GETS ME SOUR...

GO ON HOME. GOT AN ERRAND TO RUN.

HEH HEH... UPSIE... THERE, HEH HEH.

NOW, IN WASHINGTON...

BUT IT'S BORING.

ISN'T THERE A SINGLE PROGRAM THAT PERKS YOUR INTEREST?

WHAT ABOUT MUSIC SHOWS?

WATCHING THEM TIRES ME OUT...

BECAUSE YOU'RE NOT USED TO IT?

I GOT YOU A LOT OF BOOKS TOO, BUT YOU RARELY READ.

DIDN'T YOU, IN THE STOREHOUSE?

I USED TO ...

BUT EVERYTHING SEEMED TO BE ABOUT SOME OTHER WORLD... I LOST INTEREST.

WELL, YEAH, BACK THEN. WHAT ABOUT NOW?

AREN'T YOU BACK IN THE REAL WORLD?

...

AND YOU NEED TO START GOING OUT...

IF JUST TO SHOP.

566

567

569

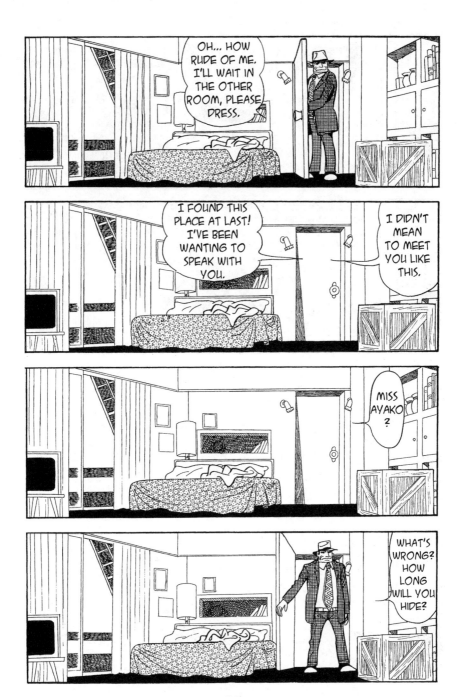

571

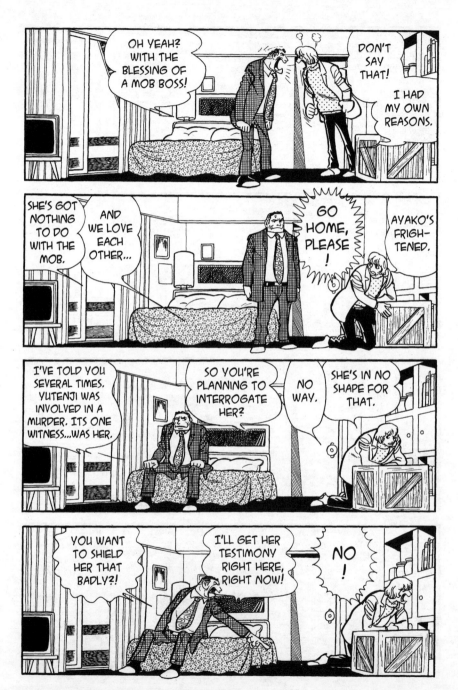

574

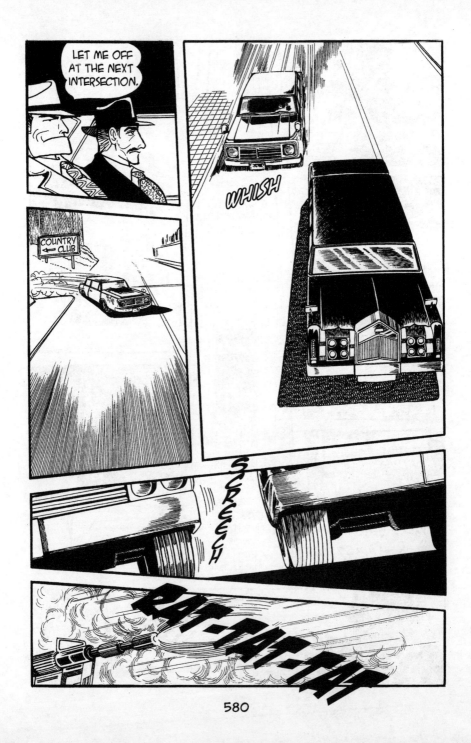

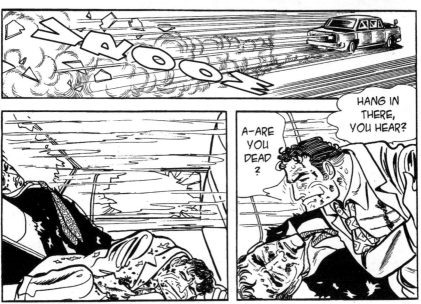

POLICE HOSPITAL

WEEEWEEOOOWEEEEEOOO

O. R.

SECTION CHIEF !!

ARE YOU ALL RIGHT, SIR?!

IT'S JUST MY ARM. THE REST IS JUST SPLATTER.

I HEARD OUSHINKAI'S YUTENJI WAS ALSO SHOT?

582

TOO EARLY TO SAY. HE HAS 12 BULLETS EMBEDDED IN HIM.

AH!

OUSHIN-KAI MEM-BERS!

THIS IS NOT GOOD.

THEY'RE GONNA GO NUTS.

CHIEF! IF YOU MOVE TOO MUCH, YOU'LL REOPEN...

...

I'LL LOOK INTO THIS INCIDENT. DON'T ANY OF YOU GO DO ANYTHING ON YOUR OWN, YOU HEAR? I'M WARNING YOU RIGHT NOW.

THIS OF ALL THINGS, WE CAN'T LET GO.

I'LL STOP YOU WITH THE FULL FORCE OF THE POLICE!

I WISH YOU'D SAID THOSE WORDS TO THE ICHOUKAI EARLIER!

DO YOU HAVE ANY EVIDENCE THAT THEY WERE BEHIND THE ATTACK?

DON'T NEED ANY. IT HAS TO BE MORIDEN.

WON'T YOU JUST LOOK THE OTHER WAY THIS ONE TIME, NO MATTER WHAT?

NO!

I'LL ISSUE ARREST WARRANTS IF I HAVE TO!

KEEP A REAL CLOSE EYE ON ICHOUKAI AND OUSHINKAI. PULL RIOT SQUADS TOGETHER.

...

AH, THE PATIENT IS REGAINING CONSCIOUSNESS...

WHAT ASTON-ISHING FORCE OF WILL.

THAT WAS CLOSE, EH?

DO YOU THINK IT WAS ICHOUKAI HITMEN?

...

FATHER!

HANAO!

586

JIRO BIG
BROTHER
...

...

POLICE SIRS, THIS IS A BIG NUISANCE. WE'RE AT PEACE HERE. WON'T YA WITHDRAW?

DIDN'T OUR BOSS TELL YA THAT HE KNOWS NOTHIN'?

THAT'S NOT GOING TO MOLLIFY THE OUSHIN-KAI.

'COURSE NOT. AND IF THEY COME AT US, WE'LL FIGHT BACK.

ESPECIALLY CONSIDERIN' THAT THEY OWE US ONE.

A SCUFFLE'S BROKEN OUT WITH OUSHINKAI NEAR MISUMI-BASHI!

GAH, MISUMIBASHI? WE COMPLETELY READ IT WRONG!

BLAM

BLAM

BLAAM

ON MARCH 22, 5 INNOCENT BYSTANDERS GOT CAUGHT UP AND BECAME CASUALTIES.

A BATTLE WITHOUT HONOR OR HUMANITY LIKE HIROSHIMA'S YAMAMURAGUMI INCIDENT.

OBLIVIOUS TO IT ALL, TOMIO YUTENJI DRIFTED ON THE BRINK OF DEATH AT THE HOSPITAL.

NOTE: THE "YAMAMURAGUMI INCIDENT" ALLUDES TO AN ACTUAL YAKUZA WAR THAT INSPIRED A SERIES OF FILMS UNDER THE UMBRELLA TITLE *BATTLES WITHOUT HONOR AND HUMANITY*.

YET THE CONFLICT REVEALED UNSOUGHT TRUTHS.

PANT

PANT

PANT

PANT

PANT

NOW SPILL IT ALL! YOU SHOT THE BOSS WITH THIS GUN, DIDN'T YOU?!

WE'VE GOT ALL THE EVIDENCE!

YOU TARGETED YOUR OWN BOSS DESPITE YOUR PLEDGE TO OUSHINKAI!

WHATEVER GRUDGE YOU BEAR, HOW GANGSTER MORALS HAVE FALLEN!!

YOU LOUT, WILL YOU GIVE IT UP ALREADY?! QUIT WASTING OUR TIME!

HE'S EXERCISED HIS RIGHT TO REMAIN SILENT FOR 4 DAYS ALREADY.

GANGSTER OR RED ARMY, YOUTHS ARE SIMILAR THESE DAYS.

HEY, YOU REMEMBER MY FACE, DON'T YOU?

I'M POSITIVE YOU'RE THE FELLOW WHO SNUCK INTO THE BOSS'S HOUSE TO RAPE THE WOMAN THERE.

I KICK YOU OUT OF THERE, AND YOU TAKE IT OUT ON YOUR BOSS? MUDDLED VENGEANCE, THAT.

...

HEY!!

I KNOW SOMEONE PROMPTED, OR RATHER, ORDERED YOU TO IT.

WAS IT MORIDEN? SOMEONE FROM THE YAMANONAKA-GUMI? QUIT STALLING!!

HE'S PRETTY AGITATED. HE MAY CONFESS WITH A BIT MORE PRODDING.

OH!!

DAMN!!

YOU STUPID LOUT!!

IMITATING THE RED ARMY'S MORI?!

HE'S BEEN DEAD ABOUT 3 HOURS. IT'S TOO LATE.

HE DIDN'T LEAVE A WILL?

NO, BUT HE LEFT THIS ON THE WALL,

USING CHARCOAL OR SOMETHING.

Koto Ward
2-4 Shinsuna
K asked me
I'm sorry

Koto Ward
2-4 Shinsuna
K asked me
I'm sorry

NEEINAR NEEINAR NEEINAR NEEINAR

THIS MUST BE WHAT IT FEELS LIKE TO "GRASP AT STRAWS."

THIS IS IT. 2-4...

ALL THERE IS HERE IS THAT FACTORY SHACK.

SEEMS EMPTY ...

TRAMP

TRAMP

CREEAK
CREEAK

DO YOU SMELL THAT?

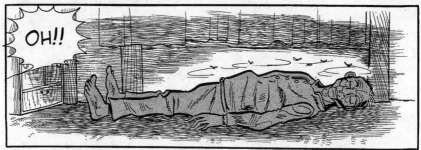

OH!!

PRETTY BAD ...

HE'S BEEN DEAD QUITE A WHILE.

HE DIED ABOUT 2 WEEKS AGO. CAUSE OF DEATH IS POTASSIUM CYANIDE. WERE ANY VIALS NEARBY?

THEN WAS IT SUICIDE? OR...

IT COULD HAVE BEEN EITHER.

TOO MANY OLD FOLK ARE DYING WITHOUT ANYONE KNOWING.

HMM, 2 WEEKS AGO WOULD BE 3 DAYS BEFORE CHIEF WAS ATTACKED.

DO YOU THINK THAT HOODLUM WHO HUNG HIMSELF SAW THIS OLD MAN ALIVE?

HOW ARE YOU FEEL-ING?

HA HA... I STILL HAVE THE DEVIL'S OWN LUCK.

SAY, MISTER TENGE, DO YOU KNOW THIS OLD MAN?

AT ANY RATE, I WISH YOU WOULDN'T DETAIN MY PARTNER KINJO WITHOUT DUE CAUSE.

NO...

WAIT... LET ME TAKE ANOTHER LOOK.

THERE'S SOMETHING FAMILIAR ABOUT HIM... THOSE EYES...

AGES AGO... RIGHT, I FEEL LIKE I SAW THAT FACE A REAL LONG TIME AGO...

JIRO HAZILY RETRACED MEMORIES FROM OVER 20 YEARS EARLIER AND BUMPED UP AGAINST THAT ACCURSED CASE... AGAINST A CERTAIN DAY BACK WHEN HE GOT DRAGGED INTO THE YODOYAMA INCIDENT.

YOU'RE WITH LT. FRED KINOSHITA?

I DON'T KNOW ANY SUCH PERSON. MY BOSS IS MAJOR CANON.

I'M KATO. MAJOR CANON IS A BIG SHOT WITH A LOT OF PULL AT CIC.

MORE THAN THAT, YOU NEED NOT KNOW.

I JUST PASS ON YOUR ORDERS.

ON THE 17TH, A MAN WILL GET OFF A TRAIN THAT PULLS IN AT 6:20PM. YOU WILL TAKE THIS MAN TO A CERTAIN LOCATION...

AND THEN RETURN IN 30 MINUTES. THERE WILL BE A CAR PARKED WITH A CORPSE INSIDE IT. DRIVE IT...

AND DUMP THE BODY ONTO THE DESIGNATED TRACKS AT 8:15.

A TRAIN WILL PASS THROUGH AT 8:20. MAKE IT LOOK LIKE HE WAS RUN OVER.

HERE'S A PICTURE OF THE MARK AND A MAP.

WE'LL PROBABLY NEVER MEET AGAIN.

BE CARE- FUL.

THAT'S IT! HE'S THE MAN FROM THAT DAY!!

I COULDN'T FORGET HIM IF I TRIED... THAT EXPRESSIONLESS, COLDHEARTED LOOK... THE MAN WHO CALLED HIMSELF KATO!

MISTER TENGE, DID YOU REMEMBER SOMETHING?

N-NO...

CHAPTER 18

THE HUMAN CIRCUIT

SPRING BE IN FULL BLOOM NOW...

LOOK AT YOU, YOU'VE GOTTEN GRAYER, KINJO.

HO HO HO... THAT AIN'T NEW.

IT'S ALREADY BEEN **22** YEARS SINCE I TEAMED UP WITH YOU... TIME FLIES.

YOU KNOW, THIS LAST TO-DO HAS CONVINCED ME THAT I'M UTTERLY FED UP WITH THIS LIFE. I'M THINKING ABOUT CALLING IT QUITS.

DON'T LOSE HEART, BOSS, NOT AT THIS CRUCIAL TIME.

EVERYTHING I'VE BEEN ABLE TO ACCOMPLISH IS THANKS TO YOU. TAKE OVER THE OUSHINKAI WHEN I RETIRE.

I'M ONLY A RIGHT-HAND MAN. A WIFE AIN'T GOOD AT DOING A HUSBAND'S JOB, HA HA...

I HAVE A FAVOR TO ASK OF YOU.

ONE LAST INDUL-GENCE.

?

GIVE YANAGIDA 100 MILLION.

YANA-GIDA?

POLITICAL CONTRI-BUTIONS AGAIN, BOSS?!

I THOUGHT I WARNED YOU TO QUIT WASTIN' YOUR MONEY!

BESIDES, THEY'RE PROJECTIN' DEFEAT FOR YANAGIDA IN THE UPCOMIN' ELECTION.

I'VE GOT MY REASONS FOR IT.

I WANT TO GET MONEY TO YANAGIDA AND THEN ASK HIM SOME THINGS!

LET US TOAST TO YOUR RECOVERY, MISTER YUTENJI...

AND TO YOU GETTING ELECTED, YANAGIDA SENSEI.

THE PARTY CHAIR DEEPLY APPRECIATES YOUR CONTRIBUTION... HE'S DIRECTED ME TO COMPENSATE YOU IN SOME WAY.

IF THERE'S ANYTHING I CAN DO FOR YOU, LET ME BE OF ASSISTANCE.

I'M VERY GRATE- FUL.

ACTUALLY, WEREN'T YOU WITH THE RAILWAYS BUREAU, TRANSPORT MINISTRY, JUST AFTER THE WAR?

YES, INDEED. I WORKED UNDER MISTER KAGAYAMA.

WERE YOU TIGHT WITH JNR PRESIDENT SHIMOKAWA TOO?

HMM...

SHIMOKAWA... HE WAS CLOSE TO TRANSPORT MINISTER OHYA, BUT ME, I ONLY MET HIM A FEW TIMES.

I'VE HEARD YOU BECAME ACQUAINTED WITH MAJOR GENERAL WILLOUGHBY OF GHQ GENERAL STAFF THROUGH SHIMOKAWA.

WHY ARE YOU ASKING SUCH THINGS?

SURE, I RECALL MEETING WILLOUGHBY AT A PARTY, BUT THAT'S ABOUT IT. I DON'T REMEMBER MUCH BEYOND THAT.

SOME- HOW, I DON'T THINK THAT'S ALL.

605

YOU...

YOU DARE... THREATEN ME?

IF YOUR SECOND SET OF BOOKS IS MADE PUBLIC, YOUR CAREER WILL GO POOF...

I KNOW WHO YOU ARE NOW, YOU SCOUNDREL!

FOR YOUR OWN SAKE,

I SUGGEST YOU ANSWER MY QUESTIONS.

I WILL DO NO SUCH THING!!

VERY WELL.

LET ME PLACE A CALL TO A CERTAIN QUARTER.

WAIT!!

LOTS OF FOLKS WHO'D LIKE TO ROUGH YOU UP AND TAKE YOU DOWN.

THUMP

SPLISH

FOR HEAVEN'S SAKE, YUTENJI, JUST NOT THAT...

A TEARFUL ENTREATY THIS TIME?

QUITE A TO-DO TONIGHT, MA'AM.

I AIN'T HEARD A THING.

ME NEI-THER.

BETTER NOT TO KNOW.

ALL RIGHT!

MAJOR GENERAL WILLOUGHBY... REALLY HAD IT IN FOR GHQ'S GOVERNMENT SECTION... AND ON ORDERS FROM A KEY PENTAGON FIGURE, HE PERSISTED IN SABOTAGE.

I HEARD HE TARGETED JAPANESE AND AMERICANS ALIKE WITH RUTHLESS YET INGENIOUS PLOTS...

SEEMS LIKE THERE WERE MANY U.S. CASUALTIES, TOO.

WAS HE BEHIND THE SHIMOKAWA AND MATSUKAWA INCIDENTS?

I-I DON'T KNOW. I KNOW NOTHING ABOUT THAT. I'M COMPLETELY IGNORANT ABOUT ANY SPECIFICS!

IT'S THE TRUTH!

BUT...

BUT...?

THERE WERE TWO JAPANESE WORKING UNDER WILLOUGH-BY...

WHO OUGHT TO KNOW THE TRUTH.

WHAT ARE THEIR NAMES?

I-I BELIEVE... ONE WAS NISEI, A KINOSHITA, I THINK...

LIEUTENANT FRED KINOSHITA!

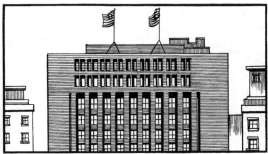

JIRO TENGE, RIGHT?! I'VE BEEN AWAITING YOU. I'M LT. FRED KINOSHITA.

COLONEL RESTON WAS AN ACADEMY CLASSMATE OF MY BOSS, MAJOR GENERAL WILLOUGHBY.

THE BIGWIGS MUST TRUST YOU.

AND MY TASK?

...

WAIT, I DIDN'T CATCH THAT. WHO DID YOU SAY WAS THE OTHER JAPANESE?

WHAT ?!

ARE YOU SURE THAT WAS THE NAME?

I NEVER KNEW HIS FACE, BUT HIS NAME I REMEMBER CLEARLY!

BOSS
!!

WHAT'S THE MATTER?
YANAGIDA MUST'VE
BEEN JUBILANT!

I JUST FOUND OUT THE NAME OF THE FELLOW WHO FORCED ME INTO A TWENTY-YEAR LIFE ON THE RUN...WHO DERAILED MY LIFE!!

WHAT?

KINJO, THAT PUNK WHO SHOT ME WAS DEFINITELY MANIPULATED BY SOMEONE ELSE...

HE HAD KATO KILLED, THEN TRIED TO ERASE ME, TOO.

DO YOU KNOW WHY?

THOSE ACCURSED INCIDENTS 23 YEARS AGO...

THIS PERSON IS TRYING TO ELIMINATE EVERYONE WHO WAS INVOLVED! AFTER ALL THESE YEARS!

HE WAS AN AGENT OF GHQ'S MAJOR GENERAL WILLOUGHBY... AND COOKED UP THE YODOYAMA INCIDENT!

I DON'T KNOW THE EXACT NUMBER, BUT HE CAUSED DOZENS TO DIE.

YET HE'S WALKING ABOUT ALL HAPPY-GO-LUCKY...

YOU SEE, I WANT TO ASK HIM

WHY... WHY HATCH SUCH STUPID PLOTS?

I FOUND A CERTAIN NOTEBOOK INSIDE YOUR SAFE...

WITHIN WHICH WERE RECORDED SEVERAL DATES AND NAMES

INCLUDING THAT OF KATO AND MYSELF!

MY DATE WAS THE DAY I WAS SHOT!

YOU WERE CARE-LESS.

BUT SO WAS I, NOT TO THINK THAT IN MY OWN...

KLUNK

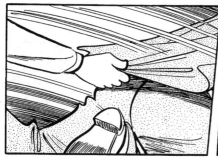

NOW SPEAK. I'M GOING TO MAKE YOU SPILL IT ALL, KINJO...

616

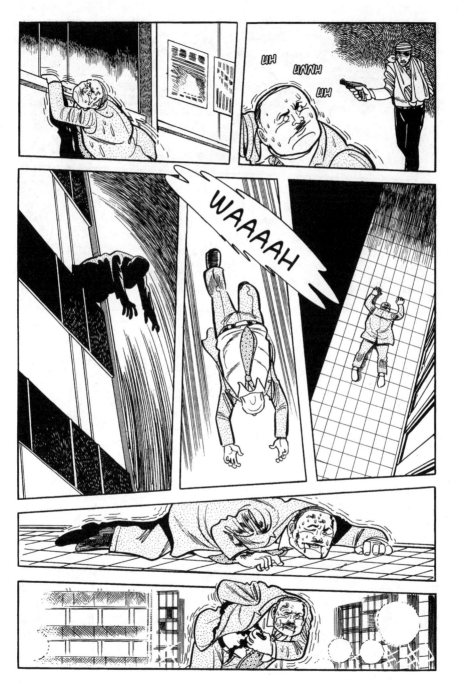

OH... MISTER YUTENJI...

ARE YOU WELL ENOUGH TO BE OUT?!

YEAH, SINCE SOME DAYS AGO.

JIRO BIG BROTHER...

IT'S BEEN YEARS SINCE YOU CALLED ME THAT.

HOW'S SHE DOING?

SHE'S GETTING USED TO NORMAL LIFE...

BUT NOW AND THEN ODD HABITS...

THAT'S FINE. SHE'LL LEVEL OUT.

I'M GOING TO BE TAKING A TRIP.

A TRIP?

DOES MY FATHER KNOW?

PROB-ABLY...

ONCE MY BUSINESS IS DONE, I'LL RETURN.

STAY WELL UNTIL THEN, AYAKO.

BRRRNG

YES, THIS IS HANAO...

WHAT?!

...

MISTER YUTENJI...

MY FATHER JUST CALLED TO TELL ME NOT TO LET YOU LEAVE.

620

A WARRANT HAS BEEN ISSUED FOR YOU FOR CRIMINAL INTIMIDATION AND MURDER... WHAT DID YOU DO?!

I KILLED KINJO... LAST NIGHT.

YOUR RIGHT-HAND MAN?

HAVE YOU LOST YOUR MIND? WHY?!

HE WAS THE ONE WHO SENT THAT PUNK TO ERASE ME.

I WAS GRILLING HIM ABOUT IT WHEN I ACCIDENT- ALLY KILLED HIM.

YOU'RE IN A BAD BIND.

TAKING A TRIP... FLEEING WILL MAKE IT WORSE.

621

BUT THERE ARE STILL SO MANY THINGS THAT I WANT TO KNOW!

UNTIL I DO, I NEED YOUR FATHER TO HOLD OFF.

NO TIME TO EXPLAIN.

MY FATHER TOLD ME TO KEEP YOU FROM LEAVING!

STAY OUT OF OTHER PEOPLE'S BUSINESS, STRIPLING!

EVEN IF YOU RUN, YOU'LL BE ARRESTED. PLEASE TURN YOURSELF IN!

ARE YOU LECTURING ME?

YOU OUGHT TO JUST CONCERN YOURSELF WITH AYAKO. JUST FOCUS ON MAKING HER HAPPY!!

IT'S ALL RIGHT FOR YOU TO MAKE HER UNHAPPY BY GOING ON THE LAM?!

THAT WASN'T PART OF OUR DEAL.

I DON'T CARE IF YOU'RE A BUDDING PROSECUTOR, DON'T TALK FRESH!

I TOLD YOU AYAKO WOULD BE MISERABLE IF SHE STAYED WITH YOU.

623

HANAO!

FATHER... SORRY. HE GOT ME GOOD ...

YEAH, IT'S ME, GETA!

PUT YUTENJI ON THE NATIONAL WANTED LIST! THAT'S RIGHT, HE'S A FLIGHT RISK.

ON JUNE 2, 1972, METRO POLICE INVESTIGATIONS SECTION ONE PUT OUSHINKAI CHAIRMAN TOMIO YUTENJI ON THE NATIONAL WANTED LIST FOR THE MURDER OF GANG BRASS GOSEI KINJO. COINCIDENTALLY, DPP DIET MEMBERS LOOKING INTO THE MONEY TRAIL OF THE YANAGIDA FACTION HAD ZOOMED IN ON YUTENJI'S NAME. THE PRESS LINKED THE TWO FOR A SPECTACULAR WRITE-UP.

FURTHERMORE, THROUGH SOME SOURCE, YUTENJI'S INVOLVEMENT IN THE YODOYAMA INCIDENT 23 YEARS EARLIER WAS SCOOPED BY X DAILY.

AIEEE!!

TH-THAT'S BIG BRO !!

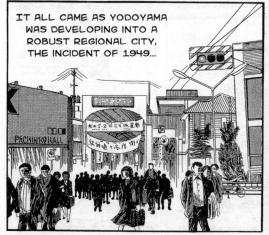

IT ALL CAME AS YODOYAMA WAS DEVELOPING INTO A ROBUST REGIONAL CITY, THE INCIDENT OF 1949...

ALL BUT FADED INTO OBLIVION.

A FEW DAYS LATER, A LONE MAN DISEMBARKED AT A SKYLINE HIGHWAY BUS STOP JUST OUTSIDE YODOYAMA.

YAH, YAH, I'D NEV'R FERGET THAT BACK O' HIS.

HURRY, CHASE AFTER HIM FER ME. I JUST AIN'T ABLE T'RUN...

BE THIS YAMAZAKI CLINIC? THIS BE TENGE, BUT WOULD OUR HOUSE HEAD PERCHANCE BE OVER THERE?

I'D LIKE T'BORROW YER PHONE.

CIGARETTES

WHAT UP, SHIRO? COME AGAIN?

DAT FER REAL?

KACHINQ

JIRO'S COME BACK...

JIRO?!

WHAT SHOULD I DO?

HOW'D HE SEEM T'YA?

I AIN'T SEE HIM. MA DID.

ALWAYS BOTHERED ME HE MIGHT RETURN SOME DAY, THO'.

SO THIS TOMIO YUTENJI FELLA REALLY BE JIRO?

YEAH. MA BE CONVINCED JIRO BE DA ADMIRABLE LOUT DAT'S BEEN SENDIN' AYAKO MONEY LIKE CRAZY.

'N TH' FELLA IN THIS NEWSPAPER PHOTO LOOKS JUST LIKE HIM... SO IT BE QUITE LIKELY.

BUT EITHER WAY, I AIN' WANNA HAVE ANYTHIN' T'DO WIT' EITHER JIRO O' AYAKO NO MORE!

DOC, YA BE A WISE MAN, THINK UP A WAY T'CHASE JIRO OFF WIT'OUT DA POLICE O' NEWS FOLKS FINDIN' OUT!

HO HO, YA ALWAYS BRING YER BOTHER- SOME PROBLEMS T'ME.

'N YET...

IF YUTENJI REALLY BE YER LI'L BROTHER...

HE GOTS TONS O' MONEY. THIS PAPER SAYS HE BEEN CONTRIBUTIN' T'POLITICOS IN ADDITION T'SENDIN' AYAKO 10'S O' MILLIONS.

YA MIGHT WELL BE ABLE T'RESTORE TH' TENGE GLORY.

DEMAND GRATITUDE FROM JIRO 'N SHELTER HIM!!

634

FOOL, IF WE DO SUCH A THING 'N TH' POLICE CATCH ON, WE BE DONE FER!!

IF IT BE ALL RIGHT WIT' YA, I'LL TALK T'JIRO ON MY OWN.

BUT, WHATEV'R LOAD I GET FROM JIRO BE ALL MINE.

BUT...

YA SEE, ICHIRO, "DISCRETION" ALSO MEANS TAKE A CHANCE WHEN YOU MUST.

THIS BE TH' PERFECT OPPORTUNITY T'GET YER HANDS ON LOTS O' DOUGH... 'N YA BE HIS BIG BRO TOO!

I JUST CAN' MUSTER NO DISCRETION RIGHT NOW!

FARMIN' I BE CONFIDENT 'BOUT, BUT THIS CHARTIN' TH' COURSE O' TENGE BE SUCH A BURDEN T'ME!

NOW LISTEN UP.

THERE BE THIS COAL STORAGE CAVE IN OKUNOSAWA. ITS ENTRANCE BE HIDDEN FROM SIGHT BY FERNS 'N UNDERGROWTH. WE OUGHTA STASH HIM IN THERE T'START, BRING HIM FOOD 'N EFFECTS ...

AIN' IT. YER PA WAS A GREAT MAN, IF YA THINK ON IT.

JUNE 19TH. IN HOT AND HUMID YODOYAMA REVERBERATED THE HOARSE SINGING OF PINE CICADAS. TOWARDS THE BACK OF A TREE GROVE IN THE FOOTHILLS WAS A SMALL CEMETERY. A LONE WOMAN CROUCHED QUIETLY IN FRONT OF THE GRAVE OF YODOYAMA INCIDENT VICTIM TADASHI ENO.

LONG TIME NO HELLO, TADASHI...

I'VE... AGED SINCE I WAS LAST HERE.

NOW DON'T GET ANGRY AT ME FOR MARRYING SOMEONE ELSE AND FOR MY MUNDANE LIFE. I'VE NEVER FORGOTTEN ABOUT YOU FOR **20-ODD** YEARS.

I STILL LOVE YOU, VERY MUCH.

THIS WHOLE TIME...

DAY AFTER DAY...

I'VE THOUGHT ONLY ABOUT REVENGE, AGAINST YOUR KILLERS.

I EVEN DREAM ABOUT IT, TADASHI.

THIS MAN YUTENJI WAS AMONG THOSE WHO KILLED YOU!

THAT'S RIGHT, MA'AM.

WHO... ARE YOU?!

TOMIO YUTENJI. A MAN WHO WAS ONCE YOUR BROTHER.

JIRO BIG BROTHER?!

THAT WE WOULD MEET HERE LIKE THIS, BY CHANCE... PERHAPS YOUR LOVER BROUGHT US TOGETHER.

T-TOMIO YUTENJI? IT REALLY WAS YOU?

THAT'S RIGHT, AND LET ME BE CLEAR. I WAS THE ONE WHO LEFT TADASHI ENO ON THE TRAIN TRACKS TO BE RUN OVER, 23 YEARS AGO.

...

M-MURDER-ER!!

I'LL SAY IT AGAIN. IT WAS I WHO HAD A TRAIN RUN OVER YOUR LOVER TADASHI ENO.

CHAPTER 19

DARKNESS

TADASHI
ENO

THAT, I AM NOT. DON'T JUMP TO CONCLUSIONS.

HE WAS DEAD BY THAT TIME.

I CAUSED ENO TO BE RUN OVER, BUT IT WAS A CORPSE THAT I LUGGED ONTO THE TRACKS.

ENO HAD BEEN KILLED BY SOMEONE ELSE BEFOREHAND!

I WAS PART OF A CERTAIN ORGANIZATION BACK THEN, ONE ASSEMBLED BY GHQ. I WAS MERELY FOLLOWING ORDERS.

JIRO BIG BRO!

BACK THEN I WAS A LOOSE CANNON, NEGATIVE ABOUT EVERYTHING... I DIDN'T CARE WHO I WAS WORKING FOR OR WHO GOT HURT.

YOU WERE INVOLVED WITH DPP'S YODOYAMA CHAPTER THEN— BECAUSE ENO BELONGED TO THE PARTY.

AT FIRST, I THOUGHT IT WAS ALL A CUNNING AMERICAN PLOY TO SUPPRESS THE LEFT WING. STAGING VARIOUS INCIDENTS AND MAKING THE POPULACE THINK THE LEFT WING WAS CAUSING MAYHEM TO INCITE A REVOLUTION IN JAPAN... THAT WOULD PROVIDE AN EXCUSE TO START A RED HUNT.

BUT WHEN I THOUGHT ABOUT IT MORE DEEPLY, IT DIDN'T MAKE SENSE. WITHIN GHQ, THERE WAS BAD BLOOD BETWEEN GENERAL STAFF AND GOVSEC. I STARTED WONDERING IF MY ORGANIZATION WAS FORMED BY A FACTION IN GHQ, JUST LIKE THERE ARE HAWKS AND DOVES IN THE AMERICAN GOVERNMENT. BUT, NAOKO! IT WAS MUCH MORE THAN THAT...

A LOT OF PEOPLE WHO WERE INVOLVED IN THOSE INCIDENTS ARE STILL OUT THERE LIKE ME. AND NOW, FOR SOME REASON, WE ARE BEING ERASED ONE BY ONE. MY LIFE, TOO, WAS TARGETED. WHY?

AS WE SPEAK, U.S. FORCES ARE WITHDRAWING FROM VIETNAM, AND RELATIONS WITH CHINA ARE THAWING... AMERICA HAS DRASTICALLY CUT FOREIGN AID.

ALL AT THE SAME TIME.

WHY?

THE ORGAN MUST'VE BEEN DISBANDED... AND NOW THEY'RE CLEANING UP.

THEY'RE TYING UP LOOSE ENDS. WHAT A HASSLE FOR ME.

I...

AM GOING TO AMERICA.

I'LL FERRET OUT THEIR IDENTITY. IT MAY BE A DOOMED VENTURE, BUT I'M GOING TO TRY.

646

647

THEN STAB ME...

UNTIL YOU'RE HAPPY.

BROTHER! STABBING YOU ISN'T GOING TO BRING HIM BACK!

TZTZZ
TZTZZ

TZTZZ
TZTZZ

TZTZZ
TZTZZ

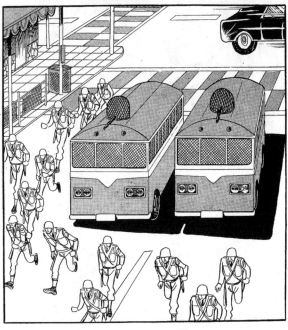

NO ONE FITTIN' YUTENJI'S DESCRIPTION HAS SHOWN UP ON OUR RADAR YET. MAYHAP HE DISGUISED HIMSELF.

WHEN I HEARD HE BE HEADIN' TOWARDS YODOYAMA, I THOUGHT JIRO TENGE WOULD DROP BY HIS BIRTH HOME BEFORE TAKIN' FLIGHT.

I'VE SENT SOME PLAIN-CLOTHES T'HIS FAMILY HOME.

IT'S SWELTERING IN HERE.

OUR AIR CONDITIONER'S BROKEN. SORRY ABOUT THAT.

THIS ONCE WAS MISTER TANUMA'S FAN. PLEASE FEEL FREE TO USE IT.

AH, PRICE-LESS!

HANAO!

WHERE'S HE TAKEN HIMSELF?

MY SON IS HERE WITH AYAKO...

HO!

YOU KNOW, THE YOUNGEST TENGE CHILD.

PERHAPS THEY'VE GONE TO AYAKO'S HOME.

HOW CAREFREE OF YOUNG FOLK, WHEN WE'RE ON HIGH ALERT....

HUFF

HUFF, HUFF

MA'AM, WHAT'S ...

OH... YER... IF IT AIN' NAOKO?!

WHAT? NAOKO BIG SIS?

HEY, SIS!! WHY YA SUDDENLY COME T'YODO- YAMA?

OH... SHIRO? I-I'M SO GLAD TO SEE YOU...

I-IT'S JIRO BIG BROTHER ...

WHAT?!

I-I WAS AT THE CEMETERY, PAYING MY RESPECTS... WHEN JIRO SHOWED UP.

JIRO? WHERE HE AT?

OH!

I ASKED YA WHERE JIRO BE!!

HE'S INJURED AND COLLAPSED IN THE CEMETERY. HE'S BLEEDING BADLY. DOC, PLEASE, GO STOP HIS BLEEDING!

HE BE WOUNDED 'N DOWN? THAT AIN' GOOD.

PLEASE, DOC, COULD YOU TREAT HIM QUIETLY, IN SECRET?

I KNOW, I KNOW. JIRO STILL BE A TENGE. I'LL MAKE SURE TH' POLICE DON' CATCH ON...

WE'LL GO 'N TAKE JIRO T'A REAL CLEVER HIDIN' PLACE.

MM-HMM. I'LL TREAT 'N LET HIM RECOVER, THERE.

SHIRO! YA COME LATER. BUY THOSE THINGS I MENTIONED AT TH' STORE FIRST 'N BRING THEM WIT' YA.

YAH...

LET'S GO, NAOKO.

BE YA TH' REASON BEHIND AYAKO BEIN' MISSIN'?

I LOOKED ALL O'ER TOKYO FER HER, DAMMIT!

AYAKO, COME HOME WIT' ME. MA BE WAITIN' THERE FER US.

NOT YET!!

WHAT ...?

HEY, WE BE HAVIN' A FAMILY CONVERSATION HERE!

TOMIO YUTENJI'S HERE IN YODOYAMA! ONLY AYAKO CAN GET HIM TO TURN HIMSELF IN. HE'LL FOLD AND SHOW HIMSELF IF AYAKO APPEALS TO HIM... THAT'S WHY I BROUGHT HER! OTHERWISE, SHE'D STILL BE IN TOKYO.

IN THAT CASE, I KNOW WHERE HE BE.

I AIN' MIND TELLIN' AYAKO, BUT I SURE AIN' LETTIN' A STRANGER IN ON IT!

656

YOU KNOW WHERE YUTENJI IS?

IF YOU DON'T TELL ME, YOU'LL BE GUILTY OF HARBORING A FUGITIVE.

WOW, YA ACT LIKE YA ACTUALLY KNOW WHAT YA BE SAYIN'.

I SAID I KNEW WHERE HE BE AT, NOT THAT I WERE SHELTERIN' A CRIMINAL!

AYAKO GONNA BE TALKIN' HIM DOWN, SO I'LL TELL HER... BUT I AIN' NEED T'TELL YA.

YOU'RE QUITE ARGUMEN-TATIVE.

ALL RIGHT... WHAT ABOUT THIS?

LET'S USE THE RED ARMY AND MAFIA WAY OF TAKING FOLK TO THEIR HIDEOUTS.

A BLINDFOLD. SEE, NOW I WON'T KNOW WHERE WE'RE GOING.

FINE. GET IN.

AYAKO, SIT UP FRONT.

WE THERE YET?

IT FEELS LIKE WE'RE DEEP IN THE MOUNTAINS.

DON' YA DARE TAKE YER BLINDFOLD OFF!

I WON'T... BUT THE SMELL OF FRESH LEAVES IS AWESOME...

YOU DON'T GET THIS IN TOKYO AT ALL.

YA CAN TAKE IT OFF NOW... WE BE HERE.

THIS BE A COAL STORAGE CAVE.

HARD T'TELL FROM TH' OUTSIDE.

REMEMBER ME, YOUR BIG SISTER?

SO THIS BE AYAKO?

YA SURE TURNED INT'A FINE YOUNG LADY.

'N WHO BE YA?

AYAKO'S GUARDIAN, MY NAME IS GETA. SORRY TO INTRUDE.

ACTUALLY, WE'RE HERE TO HELP MISTER YUTENJI TURN HIMSELF IN.

I BE A PHYSICIAN, 'N I INSIST ON COMPLETE BED REST FER THIS MAN. IF TH' POLICE BARGE IN HERE O' HE OTHERWISE GETS WORKED UP, HIS TREATMENT WILL BE COMPROMISED. FIRST, HE NEEDS REST HERE 'TIL HE MAKES A COMPLETE RECOVERY.

SO YOU'RE GOING TO HARBOR A FUGITIVE?

YA MISUNDERSTAND ME. I BE SEQUESTERIN' HIM.

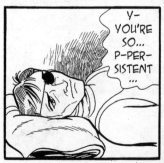

Y- YOU'RE SO... P-PER- SISTENT...

ALL OF YOU HERE ARE MR. YUTENJI'S BLOOD RELATIVES, RIGHT?

WHEN FAMILY MEMBERS SHELTER A CRIMINAL, IT'S NOT A CRIME.

BUT I'D STILL RATHER NOT GET ANY OF YOU MIXED UP IN THIS.

IT'S ALL UP TO MR. YUTENJI.

YA SURE BE MIGHTY SAUCY FER A STRIPLIN'!

EVEN IF I WEREN' FAMILY, I'D REFUSE FER HUMANITARIAN REASONS!

HUMANITARIAN REASONS? DON' MAKE ME LAUGH.

DON' YA REMEMBER, DOC YAMAZAKI?

20-ODD YEARS AGO... AT THAT FAMILY MEETIN' AT TH' HOUSE, YA SAID YA AIN' WANT TH' TENGE FAMILY PRODUCIN' ANY CRIMINALS.

ICHIRO BIG BRO... YA SAID WE COULDN' AFFORD T'HAVE OUR NAME TARNISHED.

I AIN' REMEMBER ANY SUCH THING!

YA SAY YA DON'T, BUT YA WERE TH' RINGLEADER, BRO.

YA WERE THERE TOO, JIRO BIG BRO.

'N AT THAT CLAN MEET, 'TWAS DECIDED T'OBLITERATE YER SOLE WITNESS AYAKO FROM TH' FAMILY REGISTER.

B-BUT IT COULDN' BE HELPED BACK THEN. WE AIN' HAVE NO CHOICE 'CUZ YER PA SAKUEMON...

WERE AN ABSOLUTE DICTATOR 'N WOULDN' LISTEN T'NO ONE...

DOC, YA BE SO FULL O' HOT AIR!

YA BE AN AVARICIOUS EGOIST BLINDED BY GREED, A DESPICABLE UNCLE.

I BET YA BE AFTER JIRO BIG BRO'S MONEY.

I KNEW IT. I THOUGHT IT MIGHT BE SO...

OTHERWISE, THERE BE NO WAY YA'D SHELTER JIRO BIG BRO, A WANTED MAN.

PLUS, ICHIRO BIG BRO, WIT' TH' TENGE FAMILY DECLININ', YA BE WANTIN' SOME DOUGH, TOO.

Y-Y-YA LOUT!! HOW DARE YA, YA SCAMP!!

I'LL ASK YA AGAIN. DID YA KILL SU'E?

...

YA KILLED HER WHEN SIS-IN-LAW INHERITED 80% O' PA'S FORTUNE 'N WAS GONNA LEAVE...

YA HID HER BODY IN TH' CESSPIT ON TH' WEST SIDE O' OUR PROPERTY!

EY?!

Q-QUIT YER JOKIN'!!

YA USED T'PACE AROUND THAT CESSPIT DAY IN 'N DAY OUT, ALL PALE-FACED.

SO I WENT DIGGIN' THERE ONE DAY!

I FOUND BONES WRAPPED IN OILCLOTH, SIS-IN-LAW...

I SNUCK HER BONES UP INTO TH' MOUNTAINS T'BURY 'EM.

I—I AIN' KILL HER!

THERE BE NO POINT IN KEEPIN' IT T'YERSELF ANY LONGER...

UNH... URR...

WHAT IS WRONG WITH ALL OF YOU ?!!

KILLING, GETTING KILLED!! WHY DO I HAVE TO LISTEN TO THIS? WHAT ARE YOU TRYING TO DO HERE?

RUNNING OVER MY LOVER, KILLING O-RYO AND SIS-IN-LAW... WHAT IS GOING ON?

WHAT IS IT WITH OUR BLOOD? AM I LIKE YOU ALL, TOO?

YUP!! YA ABANDONED AYAKO IN HER TIME O' NEED, SIS!

ALL O' YA APOLOGIZE T'AYAKO !!

IT AIN' POSSIBLE T'TURN BACK TH' CLOCK...

BUT AT LEAST, IN REGARDS T'THAT CLAN MEET...

YA CAN ALL GET ON YER KNEES 'N APOLOGIZE !!

WHO DO YA THINK YA BE... WHEN YA BE TH' ONE WHO VIOLATED HER LIKE A BEAST...

YA, SO I DID. I VIOLATED HER EV'RY DAY, LIKE A BEAST!

WHAT?!

SHIRO!! IS THAT TRUE?

YEAH, FER REAL...

HOW... HOW DARE YOU...

YOU HUMAN SCUM! YOU BRUTE!!

YA BE ABSOLUTELY RIGHT... I ONCE SAID I BE A DUMP IN WHICH GOT CHUCKED ALL O' TENGE'S SEWAGE.

...

WHERE YA BE GOIN'?! DON' YA BUDGE.

I BE WAITIN' A LONG, LONG TIME...

TIGHTLY HOLDIN' IT IN, ALL THESE YEARS, FER JUST A DAY LIKE THIS!!

ONCE YA ALL CONCEDE YE CRIMES 'N SAY SORRY T'AYAKO...

MY ROLE AS GARBAGE DUMP WILL BE O'ER, TOO!

HUMPH... DAT BE QUITE TH' SPEECH... B-BUT WHAT BE SO GREAT 'BOUT AYAKO?

SHE BE TH' FRUIT O' MY PA STEALIN' 'N SLEEPIN' WIT' MY WIFE!

SH-SHE NEV'R SHOULD'VE BEEN BORN IN TH' FIRST PLACE... I AIN' APOLOGIZIN' T'HER!

SAY AGAIN?! I'LL CUT OUT YOUR TONGUE...

NOW, NOW! LET'S ALL CALM DOWN 'N THINK...

FIRST O' ALL...

THIS AIN' GONNA END WELL FER ANY O' US...

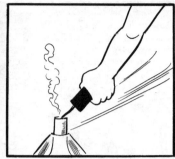

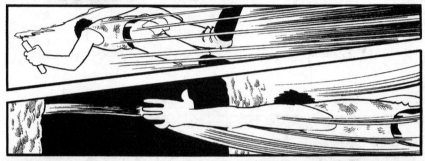

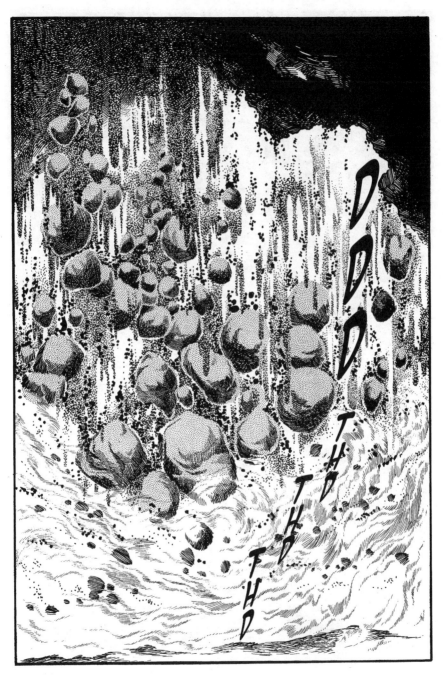

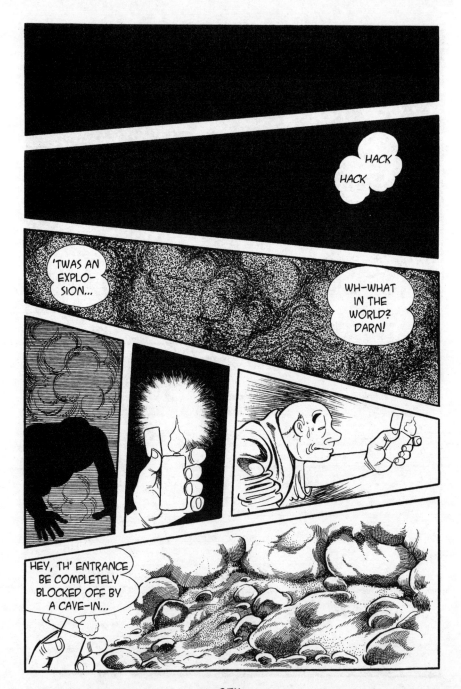

NO! SHIRO!

I SET OFF A BLAST STICK... HEH... I-I SNUCK IT ONTO TH' TRUCK ON MY WAY HERE WIT' TH' FOODSTUFF.

I WASN' PLANNIN' ON USIN' IT IF YA ALL HAD BEEN WILLIN' T'APOLOGIZE T'AYAKO...

NO ONE COULD'VE HEARD THAT BLAST ...

YA LOUT!! WHACHA GON' DO 'BOUT THIS?!

MISTA GETA, YA BE TH' ONLY STRANGER HERE.

I TRIED T'STOP YA DOWN BELOW BUT YA INSISTED, SO NOW YA BE PART O' THIS MESS...

LET'S DIG HIM OUT!

UNH... UNH...

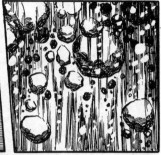

677

LEMME OUT... THIS BE A GRAVEYARD. I DON' WANNA DIE!

MR. TENGE!!

NOW LET'S JOIN FORCES AND DIG!

CAN YA... SEE MY FACE... AYAKO?

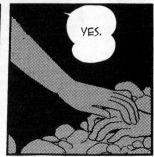

YES.

ME, I DON' SEE YA... BUT I CAN TELL IT BE YA BY YER TOUCH.

AYAKO... I MAY'VE BEEN YER BIG BRO... BUT I LOVED YA.

DON' CRY, AYAKO... TH' DARKNESS BE YER DOMAIN! YA LIVE ON, YA HEAR?

...SHIRO BIG BRO IS DEAD...

679

WHO'LL BE NEXT ?

YAMAZAKI!!

SHIRO, WHERE YA BE?!

SHIRO BIG BRO IS DEAD.

AH, H-HURRY UP 'N LEMME OUT! I-IT BE SO DARK IN HERE...

AIN' ANYONE GONNA TURN A LIGHT ON?!!

MISTER YAMAZAKI, THAT MAN'S LOST IT. LET'S IGNORE HIM AND KEEP DIGGING.

LET'S START 90 DEGREES TO THE CAVE-IN POINT, GO 3 METERS, THEN BEND AROUND IN A RIGHT ANGLE TO EXIT OUT THE CLIFF FACE.

BUT WHERE SHOULD WE DIG?

MISS NAOKO AND AYAKO, YOU TWO REACH AND PUSH TO THE SIDE ALL THE DIRT WE DIG OUT.

682

LET'S TRY THE OPPOSITE SIDE, THEN.

DON' BOTHER!! IT BE WASTED EFFORT...

MR. TENGE, IT'S TOO EARLY TO GIVE UP!!

SEE, I'VE ALREADY GOTTEN THIS FAR! DIG OUT MORE LENGTHWISE AND IT WON'T COLLAPSE.

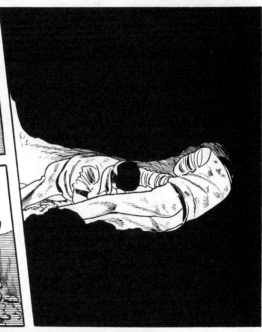

SHOW ME...

NOW LET'S KEEP DIG-GING!

WE BE DIGGIN' QUITE A WHILE. WE STILL AIN' REACH TH' OUTSIDE?

WE REALLY OUGHT TO HAVE BY NOW.

683

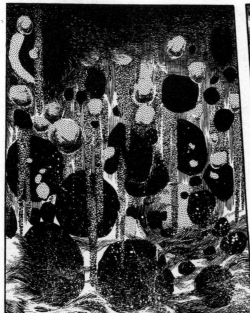

FLICKER

HERE.

AIR FROM THE OUTSIDE IS COMING IN THROUGH THIS CRACK.

LET'S DIG.

NO !!

IF THIS SPOT COLLAPSES AND THE VENT GETS PLUGGED, WE'LL REALLY BE DONE FOR.

DON'T EVEN GO NEAR IT.

LOOK... AYAKO'S LAUGHING.

HO HO HO! HO HO... HO HO HO!

HA HA HO HO HA HO HA HO HA HA HA HA HA HA HA HA

AYAKO'S LAUGHIN'. AYAKO!! THIS BE FUNNY T'YA?!

QUIT LAUGHIN', YA FOOL!

...

WHAT BE SO AMUSIN'? TELL ME, AIN' YA SCARED AT ALL?

I'M... NOT AFRAID.

I LIKE IT HERE.

IT'S JUST LIKE MY OLD ROOM.

YA MEAN THAT CELLAR?

I KNOW WHY SHE'S LAUGHING. AYAKO'S FINALLY GETTING HER REVENGE.

THE FEAR OF BEING SEALED IN FOR OVER 20 YEARS ...

YOU'RE ALL GETTING A TASTE OF IT NOW.

AYAKO MUST BE SATISFIED.

THAT'S WHY SHE'S LAUGHING.

YA WENCH!

HOW DARE YA, A LI'L LASS, MOCK YER ELDERS!

MISTER, WHERE'S THE VIGOR YOU SHOWED THAT DAY YOU JUMPED ME?

Y-YA REMEMBER THAT? I SEE... YA BE ITCHIN' T'DISGRACE ME HERE, EY!

JUST TRY LAUGHIN' AT ME AGAIN. I-I'LL KILL YA!!

RAM

AIEEE!

OH... YAMA-ZAKI'S ...!

WHO STABBED HIM?!

IT WAS ME.

MISTER YUTENJI, YOU'VE KILLED AGAIN!

IT SEEMS PRUDENT IN THIS SITUATION TO GET RID OF DANGEROUS FOLK.

EVEN IF THERE IS AIRFLOW, WE MUST WATCH OUR BREATHING.

THE FEWER PEOPLE WE HAVE, THE LONGER OUR AIR WILL LAST.

I'D LIKE TO ENSURE THAT AYAKO AT LEAST SURVIVES UNTIL THE VERY END.

WHO ARE YOU GOING TO KILL NEXT?!

YOU'RE INSANE!

CAN YOU SAY THAT YOU'RE NOT?

IF YOU THINK EVERYDAY LOGIC HOLDS IN THESE ABNORMAL CONDITIONS, THEN YOU'RE MAD.

IF WE MUST...

WE CAN EVEN EAT THE FLESH OF THE DEAD... WE'LL KEEP AYAKO ALIVE!

MY THROAT'S PARCHED. ONE DROP OF WATER IS ALL I ASK FOR.

HUSHABYE BABY, ROCK YOURSELF TO SLEEP, HUSHABYE BABY, ROCK YOURSELF TO SLEEP,

MY CUTE LITTLE BABY, WHO WAS WATCHING YOU? WHO WAS WATCHING YOU?

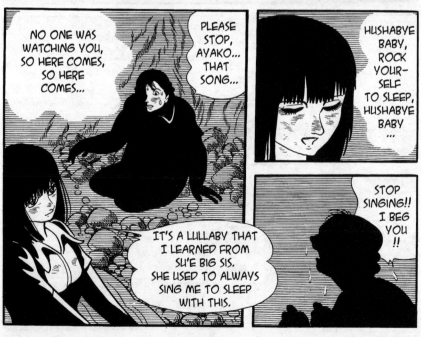

NO ONE WAS WATCHING YOU, SO HERE COMES, SO HERE COMES...

PLEASE STOP, AYAKO... THAT SONG...

HUSHABYE BABY, ROCK YOUR-SELF TO SLEEP, HUSHABYE BABY ...

IT'S A LULLABY THAT I LEARNED FROM SU'E BIG SIS. SHE USED TO ALWAYS SING ME TO SLEEP WITH THIS.

STOP SINGING!! I BEG YOU !!

ICHIRO, SHIRO, AYAKO,
AND EVEN HANAO.
NO ONE HAD A CLUE WHERE
THEY HAD DISAPPEARED TO,
AND THE SEARCH FOR THEM BY
BOTH THE POLICE AND
VILLAGERS CONTINUED
DAY AND NIGHT.

YET IT ALL
LOOKED TO
BE IN VAIN,
AS THEY SEEMED
TO HAVE
VANISHED
INTO THIN AIR.

AND SO A WEEK...
THEN TEN DAYS...
THEN TWO WEEKS
PASSED
FRUITLESSLY BY.

IN THE END,
THEY WERE ALL FOUND
QUITE BY CHANCE
THROUGH HAPHAZARD DIGGING.
BY THEN, HOWEVER,
MOST HAD ALREADY DIED
OR WERE AT DEATH'S DOOR.

AYAKO ALONE ... SURROUNDED BY A BEVY OF CORPSES...

MANAGED TO SURVIVE. HOW SHE DID SO REMAINS A MYSTERY, BUT SHE EVEN HAD A FAINT SMILE ON HER FACE ...

AYAKO !!

WE WERE TOO LATE!

AH... HANAO!

HI... FATHER...

HA HA HA HA... THAT'S WHERE OUR AIR VENT WAS...

WERE WE THAT CLOSE TO THE SURFACE? HA HA HA HA HA...

SLUMP

YA'LL BE RETURNIN' T'TOKYO PRESENTLY, MISTA INSPECTOR?

YES. I NEED TO TAKE MY SON'S BONES HOME... HOW'S AYAKO DOING?

SHE RAN OFF LAST NIGHT 'N AIN' COMIN' HOME.

WHAT?!

THAT GIRL AIN' EV'R GONNA FIT IN AT TENGE... SHE LEFT WIT'OUT A WORD.

FILE A MISSING PERSON'S REPORT! IF SHE DISAPPEARS AGAIN, WE'LL NEVER...

NAW NAW. JUST LET HER DO AS SHE LIKES...

YA SEE, MISTA INSPECTOR, WE BOTH BE OLDER 'N TIMES BE A-CHANGIN'...

YOUNG 'UNS THESE DAYS BE DIFFERENT 'N MAYHAP THAT BE ALL RIGHT.

AS FOR TH' TENGE HOUSE...

JUNE 3, 1973. IN TOKYO DISTRICT COURT,
A PAPER DELIBERATION INTO
THE LATE TOMIO YUTENJI TOOK PLACE.
THE SERIES OF ASSASSINATIONS THAT ENDED
WITH GOSEI KINJO'S MURDER WAS DEEMED
LINKED TO INTERNATIONAL ISSUES AND
TRANSFERRED TO THE JURISDICTION OF
THE MINISTRY OF FOREIGN AFFAIRS.

NOT A RUMOR REGARDING AYAKO
HAS BEEN HEARD SINCE.

THE END